Penelope Rowe was born in 1946. She has worked as a teacher, a journalist, an Opera House guide, sales rep and writer/presenter for ABC radio and SBS television.

She lives in Sydney with her three children.

▪ PENELOPE ROWE ▪

TIGER COUNTRY

Published in Great Britain by
The Women's Press Ltd 1992
A member of the Namara Group
34 Great Sutton Street, London EC1V 0DX

First published by Allen & Unwin Pty Ltd, Australia, 1990

Copyright © Penelope Rowe 1990

The right of Penelope Rowe to be identified as the
author of this work has been asserted by her in
accordance with the Copyright, Designs and Patents
Act 1988

British Library Cataloguing-in-Publication Data.
A catalogue record for this book is available from the
British Library.

This book is sold subject to the condition that it shall
not, by way of trade or otherwise, be lent, re-sold, hired
out, or otherwise circulated without the Publisher's
prior consent in any form of binding or cover other than
that in which it is published and without a similar
condition including this condition being imposed on
the subsequent purchaser.

ISBN 0 7043 4307 X

Printed and bound in Great Britain by
BPCC Hazells Ltd
Member of BPCC Ltd.

For my daughters and my beloved friends
who have walked with me
through tiger country – and beyond.

ONE

Desmond replaced the receiver and stood for a moment tugging his earlobe. Then he ran his finger around the inside of his shirt collar, easing it slightly at the front, a gesture left over from the years when he had worn a clerical collar. It relaxed him. He could breathe more freely.

'Well, that's done.' His mother looked over at him, silent. 'She said she would take the next available flight. She's coming, Mother.' Carefully he poured himself a cup of tea. 'Any lemon?' His mother walked to the fruit bowl on the other side of the kitchen. She took the lemon, sliced off a fine sliver and offered it to her son on the back of the knife. 'Thank you.' She returned to her seat in the breakfast nook and Desmond sat down opposite her. There were words to be said and he was formulating them in his mind. He wanted to make sure he said the right thing, got the tone absolutely right. No point in adding to the burden at this stage. But his mother spoke first, with an outrush of passion that made him wary.

'What's she want to come for now? We've managed, haven't we? It's trouble, trouble, trouble with her.' Her eyes glistened but she did not cry. She could not remember the last time she had cried. Had she ever cried? Desmond looked at the beautiful woman. I am in love with my mother, he thought. But the question now was, how to be fair. Fairness was important.

'I know, Mother. I know. But he's dying. He really is. There's very little time left. She does have the right to know. And he asks for her. You know that. You've heard him. You've . . .'

1

'No, Desmond, don't try to excuse her like that. I won't have it. I won't have her coming here and upsetting everybody. What has she ever done to help? It's too much. Too much.' Her tea slopped in the saucer as she picked up her cup.

'Mother, Mother.' Desmond pleaded. He was in anguish for his mother. He felt anger rise against his sister. Yes, indeed, what had she ever done? 'I had to let her know. It was the Christian...' It was the wrong thing to say. He realised it before the words were out. His mother had risen abruptly, a choked, angry groan coming from her throat, and left the room.

Desmond sat on. He sipped the tea, sucked the lemon rind, wincing at the sharp tang of it, then rinsed his cup with extreme thoroughness under the tap. Finger by finger he wiped his hands on the kitchen towel then examined his fingernails. One by one he pushed back the cuticles to encourage the perfect half moons. Desmond was proud of his hands. He believed it was his duty to keep them as perfect as possible. Not only did they dispense the Blessed Sacrament but, just as important, it showed consideration towards the faithful attending Mass. He had seen some disgusting fingernails on priests in his time, skegs hanging bloodily from torn, nicotine-stained fingers. He had been appalled and angry. It was inexcusable.

He heard his mother moving up the stairs. He was tempted to follow her, to try to explain again, but he knew this was not the time. A feeling of loneliness assailed him. Being the eldest had always meant that he was expected to be the leader. It was not easy. Again he ran his finger around his collar. The need, the longing, for that other woman rose in him. It was not one of their days for meeting. He would see her, nonetheless. She would understand. She understood everything. He looked at his watch. Five o'clock. Tuesday. How much longer would his father last? Would his sister be in time? He felt the flush of anger again. She was compounding their worries. The last thing they needed was to be worrying about whether she would arrive in time. Typical. Typical. He clenched his fists. The knuckles stood out. He moved the sinews across the knuckles. The veins popped, blue spongy. Fat, ghastly veins. He did not recall ever seeing other people with the same fat veins that his family had. But perhaps he was only imagining that. Whatever, he did not like them. He unclenched his fists.

Soon he heard his mother come back down the stairs. She re-entered the kitchen. He smiled at her. How like her. Mrs Milton had changed into a fresh dress, as she had done at five o'clock every day he could remember. Just as she had combed her hair and freshened her lipstick. The habits of years. And why not? They gave some focus to the hard days. It was good that people stuck to their habits. Desmond rose and put his arm around his mother's shoulders. He patted her cheek gently and kissed her splendid thick, white hair.

'I have to run along now, Mother. There are a few things to attend to tonight that'll keep me on the move, so you won't be able to get me. Don't worry. I'll keep in touch by phone with you. Tomorrow I'll be free all day so I'll come first thing and we'll go into the hospital together. Don't worry about Margaret now. As soon as I know her movements . . . she said she'd confirm . . . I'll organise that side of things. There's nothing to worry about. Remember that, won't you? The boys will be here soon, so you don't have to worry.' Mrs Milton tied her apron about her waist. Desmond toyed with the idea of staying. His mother's cooking was the best he had ever eaten and the company of his brothers filled him with comfort and ease. But, no. Tonight he needed the woman. He kissed his mother again. 'I'll ring in, Mother. See you tomorrow.'

Desmond unlocked the car door and slid behind the wheel. He felt no guilt that he had misled his mother. It was kinder for her to think that he had another lecture to prepare or some church function. He respected his mother utterly and knew what was permissible and what was not. She knew what priests got up to these days. She sometimes spoke with scathing bitterness on this or that example of a priest 'bringing scandal' on his calling. She had made her views clear about the immorality of the world and the laxity of the clergy in these post-Vatican Two days. It would only pain her to know. There must be no breath of scandal. The woman never spilled over into his priestly life. She lived alone in her tasteful, tidy apartment overlooking the harbour and at the ordained times he came to her. Desmond allowed the engine to idle quietly. My God, he was grateful to her. The loneliness, the physical need, the aridity of the priesthood would have destroyed him. He revved the engine, eased his foot from the clutch, checked his rear vision mirror and turned out into the street.

The call had been terminated. Still Margaret stood there, holding the receiver to her chest, hearing faintly the beep, beep, beep, the let-me-come-in, won't someone help me, cry from the telephone. Eventually she replaced the handpiece. Her eyes roamed over the flat with its huge, disordered bookshelves, elderly comfy armchairs, the bowl of yellow crocuses on the table, walls crammed with prints and family photos. We've done well, girls, she whispered, looking at a huge blown-up print of her two daughters that embarrassed them stupid every time they came home. But it was not this cosy, London flat that she was seeing. Her mind had raced ahead to the huge, dark house on the other side of the world. So now it has come, she thought. Now, after all the pain and hate, and the deadly anger, and the passage of the years, now it has come. This call that I have prepared for and dreaded and wanted.

Wanted? Yes, wanted. Have I not known that until this call came and I had the opportunity to respond, there was still unfinished business? She liked that phrase, 'unfinished business', despite its pop-psychology associations. It had tough, determined, 'here I come with my sleeves rolled up and I'm not afraid of a bit of hard work', overtones.

She crossed to the mirror. Her gaunt face stared back at her. She leaned closer and pulled her hair firmly away from her forehead. Grey hairs radiated from the roots, still not enough to call her grey-haired by any means but enough to show that she was beginning to age. Physically, yes, she was an adult. Now, I am going to find out whether or not I am grown-up.

She moved to the bedroom and, sitting down on the edge of the bed, started making a list. Her daughters laughed at the interminable lists she found so essential for order in her life. Book ticket, ring girls, ring P, cancel newspapers, cancel Gwen John rehearsal, take key next door, confirm arrival with D, give M perishables from fridge, take car to garage. She thought for a minute or so, added a few more items, then laid her list beside the phone. She pulled her case from the top of the wardrobe and started to pack her clothes.

Mrs Milton lay in the bath, lapping the hot water over her thin body. She thought with resentment about her daughter, Margaret. The girl was going to flit back into their lives after all these years while she, the mother, had never even had the opportunity to go away. Bitterness, weariness, and fury at a life of sacrifice and discipline consumed her, sapped her energy and left her an exhausted shell of despair. She kept herself going with the righteousness of anger and grasped the crumbs of pleasure that came her way.

She was soothed as she lay there in her bath which was the one truly sensual experience that she knew. Although she would not say so, she felt relief in the knowledge that the years of nursing would soon be over. Soon her husband would be dead. She thought of Desmond, her first-born, her shining child. What would she have done without him over the years? The son she gave to God. Desmond had never failed her. Desmond, the one who took over when it was too hard for her, who loved her with a gentleness and understanding that she had not found in any other man. Desmond, a priest, for whom the first woman, the only woman, was his mother. (Oh, and his sister. She refused to dwell on this.) And there were her other sons, for whom she had catered tonight, exemplary professional men, who had done well for themselves and to date shown a disinclination to marry. She could be justly proud of them.

But to think of her children meant that she must think of her daughter, and this enraged her. Every time. Every time. The girl spoiled everything. And why? Why? Why must she be different? Why must she do it her way? If her brothers could be compliant, why not she? Doing as she pleased. Disregarding family, all that was sacred, never coming home in all these years, never going to church, a divorce, heaven knows how many immoral . . . relations. Getting off scot-free! Disregarding her mother and father. Just the occasional card or photo with stilted messages from the grandchildren. Then, out of the blue, the letters that had started coming three years ago when she had heard her father was ill. A bit late then! Pathetic it had been to see his face when he had read the first one. Letters that he had wanted his wife to share. But she would not. Oh, no. Indeed she would not. If Margaret thought she could get her mother around her little finger just as she has done her father, well, she had another think coming. How dare she! Wicked! All these years when he had been starved for a word from her and it took his illness to prod her. Such was her anger that Mrs Milton sat up in her bath, tore the plug out and pulled herself up. She clenched her teeth together. Even her bath was ruined. The girl could ruin even that.

The old man lay in the hospital bed. His sons had gathered with him. His wife ministered to him. She was his lynchpin and his strength. Only one thing remained and it would be finished. I'm waiting, Matti, I'm waiting.

His mind returned to the letters, letters that had made his heart leap when he saw the writing on the envelope. She had come back to him. But why had she ever gone away? Gone away with hate blazing in her angry eyes. That he would never understand. Everything I did was for the best, Matti. You must understand that. I wanted the best for you. Can't you believe that? The best. Life's tough, I told you that, again and again. How would you have survived if you had not learned the toughness of life early on? I had to learn it. I would have achieved nothing without toughness. Look at what I was able to do. The world's no place for softies. He lifted his frail hand and brushed away tears that were running down his cheeks. He cried easily now. He was grateful his wife was not there to see them. She would guess the reason was Matti. It would upset her. But how could he help it? He needed to be sure that his daughter understood. Hurry, Matti, Hurry.

TWO

Dawn coloured the sky over Sydney. On the aircraft the cabin was made ready, the landing gear lowered, and the aircraft put itself gently down on the tarmac at Sydney airport.

Formalities, formalities, a crush of people, querulous, displaced, tired. Eventually Margaret claimed her baggage. She grasped it firmly, took a deep breath and emerged through the doors to meet her brother, Desmond. She stood before him, separated only by the handrail. She did not know whether to kiss him. *Perhaps I am afraid of you.* He smiled gravely at her and with an inclination of his head indicated that she meet him at the end of the concourse. She moved down, came around the rail and, why not, stretched up and kissed him.

'Good trip?'

'Well, you know... Desmond, how is he?'

'Fairly comfortable.'

'Can I see him now?'

'No, you're to come home first. We'll go in later.'

'But I'd like to go straight in.'

'Later. You're to come home now.' There was a bark of irritation in his voice. She felt her body prickle, a slight pulsing at the base of her skull. She nodded acquiescence and they moved to the carpark.

The trip to the family home took less than twenty minutes and as those minutes passed Margaret felt her body wind taut. She glanced at her brother. Could he hear the pounding of her heart? Deep breath in. Deep breath out...

'Okay?' asked Desmond.

'Sure. Just a bit tired, I suppose. It's a helluva flight. I'll be fine soon. Anyway, it'll be best if I can stay awake until tonight.'

Desmond drove carefully, pointing out changes to the city with the precision of a tour guide. Margaret grunted in acknowledgement. Deep breath in. Deep breath out. Then he swung smartly to the right, reduced speed to a crawl and entered the gates of Centennial Park.

'Oh! It's just the same! It hasn't changed a bit!'

'Best thing our city fathers ever did for this city,' said Desmond sternly. She glanced eagerly from left to right. The rose gardens, the duck ponds, the storm water drain, the amputee statues, and, yes, there they were, the old paperbarks with their skin lying like so much littered paper untidily around the trunks. She remembered. Deep breath in. Deep breath out.

She longed to light a cigarette. She glanced briefly at her brother.

'Okay if I smoke?'

'I'm afraid not.'

'Oh.' They emerged through the tall sandstone gates, rose over the hump and slid into the dip, down, down, until the car came to a standstill outside a tall, brick-walled house. For a moment they both sat motionless in the utter stillness of the car. A prelude of silence. Then, in unison, they swung themselves out and slammed the car doors behind them. She moved briskly to the boot of the car, hauled out her case and started for the gate.

'Here, give me that,' said her brother, reaching out.

'It's fine.'

'Give it to me.' She gave it to him.

She walked slowly down the path, looking up at the huge old house. The test, the reckoning, is starting. He's dying. Desmond walked briskly past her and slipped the key into the front door. He stood aside to let her enter, closed the door quietly and carefully behind her while she waited and then led the way to the back of the house. The kitchen. Her mother was sitting there, as beautiful as Margaret ever remembered. She was reading the paper.

'Oh, there you are.' She folded the paper. 'Desmond, put the kettle on, darling.'

'Hello,' said Margaret. She bent and kissed the soft, lined face with its high, Katharine Hepburn cheekbones. 'How are you?'

'As well as you'd expect. Your father will be pleased to see you, Margaret.'

'Yes. Um . . . well . . . when can I go in and see him? I mean, can he see people . . . whenever? Is he awake and everything.?'

'Desmond will take you in at morning tea time. You can do that, can't you, darling? It would be a great help to me.' Desmond nodded.

'No. No. I can get myself in there perfectly well. You don't have to worry. In fact, I'd like the walk. I've been sitting down for over twenty-four hours.'

'Very well. But I won't have you upsetting him, Margaret. Just remember that.' Margaret said nothing. She pushed back a sharp rejoinder. I won't upset him.

'I won't upset him,' she said finally.

Desmond handed Margaret a cup of tea. She looked at his hands as he sat down over his own cup. Consecrated hands that performed the Divine Mysteries. She disliked his hands. They were too clean. Too manicured. Almost as if a woman did them for him. The fingers were too blunt. They were her father's hands. Sadistic hands. I wonder how a cleanliness fetishist can bear to attend to his own bodily functions? What a disgusting thought. Stop it, Margaret. She shook her head against the outrageous distraction.

'How long do you intend staying, Margaret?' The daughter looked at the mother. Deep breath in. Deep breath out.

'I'll stay until he dies, and the funeral and . . . everything.'

'Ho!' A derisive laugh. 'Then off you'll go again. It's all very well for some people. Everything's easy for you, isn't it, Margaret?' Please, not now. Not now.

'Well, no, it's not really. But London's where my home is. The children, my work . . .'

'Oh, yes. This famous work. Australia not good enough for your famous work?'

'Well, I haven't had the opportunity to bring it here yet, if that's what you mean.' Don't hate me.

'Yes, well . . . I mean it, Margaret. There are to be no upsets.'

As quickly as possible. Margaret finished her tea. She showered swiftly, pulled fresh clothes from her case, wriggled into them and with a casual 'see you later', almost ran across the back garden and escaped out the back gate. She barely slowed her pace until the big house was out of sight.

Now she rummaged in her bag, grabbed the cigarettes gratefully and lit up before crossing the road. For a moment she had to pause and collect her bearings. It all looked so different. Nothing like the days when she and Aunty Ely had walked here together, she clutching Aunty Ely's hand as they passed the noisy, smelly pub and the row upon row of dark, peeling terraces with their fibro-enclosed balconies. She moved on, dodging the dog shit, until she saw the hospital, a new, gleaming hospital, ahead of her. Again she quickened her pace, strode briskly through the doors, enquired at the desk for her father and subsided against the wall of the lift as it carried her up. Deep breath in. Deep breath out.

His door was slightly ajar and there was a pencilled notice stuck lopsidedly on it. 'Family only.' She edged through the door. A man lay sleeping on the bed. White hair. White face. White sheets. White spread. White pillows. Glaring snowfields of white. A man whose breathing was sibilant and slow. And his teeth. Was this the rictus of death? His lips were drawn back over the gums and Margaret was horrified.

Then she was taken by surprise. He opened his eyes and she saw recognition dawn and a softness mist into them and he patted the bed feebly and said, quite clearly and strongly, 'Matti.'

'Oh, Daddy.' She suddenly felt pathetic and childlike and hurried over to kiss him. Tears spurted from her eyes.

'Now, now. None of that,' he said quite sternly. 'Sit down here, by me.' She pulled a chair up by the bed, her head level with his. 'Thank you for coming, my dear.'

'Oh, but of course I'd come. Of course.' Of course?

'Well, how's it all going, my dear? Your little performance, and the children? Are they well? Studying? Happy are you, Matti?' He was in a hurry to ask her. Time was short. He needed to know. Be reassured.

'Oh, yes, Daddy. I'm happy.' There was a long silence. He

closed his eyes, recovered his energy. She waited, holding herself in readiness for she knew not what. The weary old eyes reopened. He spoke with immense deliberation.

'I sometimes think, my dear, that you've never had a happy day in your life.' She stared at him, incapable of reply. Could two people, father and daughter, know so little of each other?

'Oh, Daddy, I've been very happy. My work, the children...' He shook his head impatiently on the pillow.

'Oh, yes, all that... But, well... there was all that unpleasantness... all that business when you were growing up..., He seemed agitated. 'I only wanted you, all of you, to be happy, you know.'

'Oh, I know. I do know. I am. I...' He was shaking his head feebly, his eyes never leaving her face. What was there to say?

She shifted in her chair. 'Your room looks lovely. All the flowers...'

'Yes, your mother keeps it nice.' Margaret looked around for something more to say.

'Oh, and photos, too.' Family photos, her mother, her brothers. Something was missing. Herself and her children. Each Christmas she had sent photos of the girls. Baby photos, first day at school photos, teenage photos, graduation day photos. *I will not care.*

'I've got a bag now, dear.' For a moment she did not understand.

'Oh?'

'Yes,' and he undid his pyjamas and, pulling them aside, she stared at the protuberance there. It was sudden and shocking. She felt sick.

'Oh.'

'Desmond says I shouldn't show it to anyone. But I think it helps to know. He was quite annoyed, I could tell, but I told him it was none of his business. Anyway,' he was tucking it out of sight as he spoke, thank goodness, 'they're a great improvement on the ones in my young days. Excoriated the skin all around them. Terrible. The odour too. Terrible. They tell me Sir Robert Menzies had one, and the Queen Mother, so there it is.' She nodded, smiled, still sick at the sight.

'Well, my dear, everyone's been very kind, very kind. Lots of visitors. I've always maintained that a visitor should go away feeling he's been entertained. Giving, not taking, that's what life is all about.' She nodded, only half listening to what he was saying. She did not need to listen to his philosophy now. She had learnt it by heart long ago. But how to equate this frail, gentle-looking human being on the bed with her agile, tough, commanding father? The harder she looked, the smaller, more helpless he seemed. No sign here of her creation, the war hero, the bearer of gifts, the greatest doctor, the most loving father, that she had imagined, demanded must exist in him. Here was simply an ordinary, flawed human being, now like a child who could be taken on her lap and nursed in his extremis. Here was the man she had thought was God. Now God made man. Unaccountably she saw the Pietà. The face was the same and the eyes, the eyes, sunken back into the head, surrounded by deep pools of shadow. The skull surely visible beneath the flesh. *So this is what a dying father looks like. The sorrow I feel for us both is almost too much to bear.*

And as suddenly as he had woken he dropped off to sleep again and the loud breathing started. Margaret moved with care from the chair beside the bed and crossed to the window. She leaned her forehead against the pane and stared out at the plane trees below her. She remembered. She remembered it all.

She must have sat down. Probably she dozed. Suddenly the room was full. Her mother had arrived and her brothers. The men greeted her in their undemonstrative way. But the room was too crowded. The intimacy had fled. And, above all, she must have intimacy with him if she were to be able to summon the ghosts and play the old memories once more. Go on one last journey with him.

'Does anyone stay with him at night?' she asked.

'No, the staff are marvellous.' Her mother's voice was decisive. 'It's easier for them.'

'Well, I tell you what. I can't keep awake. I'm going back to have a sleep and then I'll come in and sit with him tonight.'

'I've just told you, the staff...' Margaret was not going to listen. She needed to sit with him.

'I'll clear it with them now.' She left the room, not waiting for the argument, but as she left she saw the anger in her mother's eyes. *I make her afraid. She is jealous of him and me.*

When Margaret arrived back at the house the tiredness had gone. She felt breathless and giddy with anticipation, nervy and unable to settle into rest. She moved about the empty house. Room by room she prowled. With unconscious stealth she climbed the stairs, automatically passing over those that creaked. It was quieter up here, shuttered against the light and the noise of the traffic. She paused outside her parents' bedroom, staring in. Her eyes moved over their monumental bed with the four carved posts, and lingered on the secret panel. Her panel. She felt herself smile. She moved on. Her room! All the pinks faded now, the carpet of cabbage roses blowsy and coarse as ever she had remembered them. She shied away from the suffocation of the room and passed through to the verandah sleepout. The same filtered light through the frosted glass, the same clarity of air and space, the same branch like a shadow-puppet still performing its dance after all the years. She stood for a long time in this room. The nursery. All the babies. So lovely. Hers. Oh. She put her hand to her mouth in astonishment at the vividness of the image. Oh yes, even then I was happy. Yes.

She moved on. At the door of the study she paused again. Her eyes scanned his bookshelves, his desk, his chair, his notepaper. Her nerves jangled in a panic of memory. Her belly churned and she hurried to the toilet. As she sat hunched and furtive on the old wooden seat, the memories danced before her, testing, teasing, mocking, daring her to play. *This is what I have come for. I'm afraid.*

It was an obstacle course of memories. She faltered as she left the bathroom and turned to go down the back stairs. Of course! Hadn't Desmond written, years ago, that the back stairs had been demolished? She thought she would have liked now to go half way down those old stairs again, fingering the chiffon, trailing it in the dusty half light, a taste of sweetness on her lips, and sit alert, but secret, in the gloom.

Now, despite her tension, she persisted in her prowling, like a dentist probing for an elusive soft spot. Once the others returned the balance would change, the ghosts would hide. Back down the front staircase she went, and slowly, room by room, she walked though her childhood. There it was, the grate in the formal room, the grate where once she thought her world had finished forever. But, well, it had been different; that was all.

In the dining room she ignored the oppressive, gleaming cedar and mahogany, the glistening silver candelabra, epergnes and trays, and stood instead, close to the wall. She put her nose to the paper and sniffed. She ran her fingers down the smart striped wallpaper and felt for the secret underneath. Perhaps, just there, there'd be ... She almost laughed aloud at her foolishness. Her sentimentality. Out to the kitchen she went. She stared at the niche which once had held the black stone range. She saw the figures—her mother and herself—stirring the gravy and the white sauce. Females together. Just that once.

Suddenly she stiffened. She heard footsteps. Before she knew what she was doing she was racing, two at a time up the stairs, and crouching in the sanctuary of the verandah room. Her heart was pounding. She was shaking. How quickly the old reactions re-asserted themselves. *I am overwrought after the trip. There is nothing to be afraid of.*

Downstairs, Desmond was preparing a short, sharp speech of reprimand, certain that the occasion would arise before too long in which he would be forced to use it. Truth to be told, he found it very difficult to extend Christian charity to his sister. She caused trouble. Not to him. Not nowadays. Although she had as a child, being such a little favourite and a cry baby and apt to spoil things by not doing as he told her. In fact, that was her problem in a nutshell. She simply did not do what she was told. Had to have her own way, regardless of the inconvenience. He frowned, gritted his teeth. Their father was dying and already she had upset him. 'Where's Matti? Where is she?' On and on he'd gone, all morning, and they could tell he was unsettled. And here she was now. Coming slowly down the stairs.

'Had your sleep?'

'Well, I didn't actually go off. I just, well, I...' Her voice trailed off. She could sniff the tension between them. 'How long do they think it will be, Desmond? What do the doctors say?'

'Not long. What did you say to him? He's upset, agitated. He keeps asking for you. What did you say?'

'Nothing.'

'Look Margaret, Mother will not have him upset. It's been terribly difficult for her. It's all very well for you . . . but we've had to contend with this for so long. There are to be no upsets at this stage.'

'I've no intention of upsetting him.'

'Well, just make sure you fit in.'

'What do you mean?'

'I mean, fit in. With everyone else. Don't go off being different from everyone. Just for once, try to be a little unselfish.'

She gasped. How many years had it been since she had had this feeling? This feeling that somehow they inhabited different worlds. Years and years. And now this. She was tired and lonely. He was still talking. 'We're all rostered on to be in there. We take turns so no-one gets too tired.' He pulled a small black notebook from his pocket. 'Now, the best time for you . . .' She reasserted herself.

'Excuse me, Desmond, but I've already said what I'm going to do. I'm sitting with him tonight. Sister says that's fine, so that's that.'

'What *you're* going to do! That's all you've ever done. Suited yourself. I . . .'

'I'm sorry, Desmond.' She was cold and hard now. 'I was not aware that anything I had done had interfered with your plans in any way. I'm too tired to discuss it and furthermore, I didn't come all this way to have an argument with anyone, least of all my eldest brother whom I happen, no doubt inadequately, to love. I'm going to have a rest now and I'll go into the hospital at eight. Perhaps we can talk some more later?'

The hospital was very quiet. The visitors had left and the nigh staff were moving from room to room delivering the medication. Margaret pulled the armchair up beside the bed again. When the night nurse entered the room, her father opened his eyes.

'Not just yet, thank you, Sister,' he said firmly. He turned to his daughter. 'They try to give you that sleeping stuff and you end up sleeping all day too. Never could tolerate the stuff.... Used to tell my patients...'

'Yes, Doctor Milton. I'll come back in a little while in case you change your mind. But first I'll just give you this injection. You'll be more comfortable.'

Margaret watched as the nurse gently inserted a small needle into her father's vein. His arm looked so wasted and helpless lying on the sheet.

'What is it, Sister? Does he have a lot of those?'

'Every couple of hours. As often as needed. It keeps him comfortable. And you? Are you comfortable? Let me know if you need anything. I'll be on the nurses' station all night.'

After the sister left, the room was still.

'Well, my dear. Comfortable are you? It's good of you to come in. It gets a bit lonely at night. I don't sleep too well, you know. Gets a bit lonely.'

'I know. That's why I thought I'd like to be in here.' She saw his hand groping towards her under the covers. She leant over and took it and felt the pressure of his grip.

'It won't be long now, dear.'

'I know.'

'Your mother won't let me talk like this. She won't hear of it. But I have to say it to someone. I can say it to you. You were never a one to pull any punches. It won't be long now and there it is.' She gripped his hand tighter. He's lonely. Things to be said and no one to say them to. He had closed his eyes. The grip on her hand did not lessen.

In the dim light, unobserved, she could watch him. She saw the small unconscious movements of his lips. As though he were talking to himself. Perhaps he was. Hadn't he always? She felt the heat of tears fill her eyes. So human. A human being stripped of power, except the power of his own dying dignity.

Oh, it seemed almost too hard to bear. Too hard to bear the pain of her love and her hatred. How could he do this to her? Expose himself as a poor fragile morsel of humanity whom she could not possibly hate. He was helpless. But not too helpless to do this to her. *At last I see you as a human being. And I love you.* Love. Hate. A wild anger gripped her. She pulled her hand away in agitation. How to deal with this? All expectation turned crazy. Surges of emotion like a strong rip pulling her out from safety and certainty, threatening to drown her unless she went with it, unresisting. *I can't bear it. I can't bear it.*

Presently he opened his eyes again. Once more he groped for her hand. She gave it to him.

'Can I get you anything? A drink?' She held the glass with the bent straw to his lips. He sipped. Barely. 'Daddy, this afternoon... you said... about being happy... Please... Really... I want you to know. My life has been happy. I have so much.' He patted her hand. She felt his sympathy in the pat. She did not want his sympathy. She wanted his belief. 'Daddy. I love you. You know that, don't you?' He shook his hand, irritated, embarrassed.

'Of course, my dear.' He paused. Then, in a rush, 'Everything I did was for your own good.'

'I know. I know.'

'I've sometimes wondered, Matti...' He stopped, his face a terrible grimace. He was forcing himself on. 'I've sometimes wondered if I wasn't a little too hard on you when you were growing up.' She made a noise, unable to speak. 'But it was the only way I knew.' The pressure of his grasp was painful. 'It was for your own good. I wanted you to grow up independent, principled, upright. That's all I wanted.'

'And I have, Daddy. I have.' He jiggled her hand. Indicating? She looked into his eyes and could not read them.

THREE

Margaret-Anne Milton waits under the massive Moreton Bay fig for the tram that will take her out along the harbour front to school. While she waits she occupies herself crushing the crumbly orange figs that lie strewn over the footpath. Quickly she eats a lolly. She thinks that perhaps the eating of this lolly is a venial sin because Mummy has forbidden her to buy or eat lollies on the way to or from school.

Young Queen Elizabeth has just been coronated. 'Not coronated, silly. Crowned,' says her brother and because Margaret-Anne thinks he knows everything she agrees that it is 'crowned' but privately she always calls it 'coronated'. Her brother, Desmond, is practically the most important person in her life. They are only ten months apart in age and do most things together, though differently. Take the lollies that she is now eating. They are called 'Coronation Swaps' and every morning Desmond buys a packet solely for the two cards that are inside. He is collecting the cards because they have pictures of the kings and queens of England from William the Conqueror right up to now. The lollies are of no interest to Desmond. It is the cards he is after. A different thing altogether. Certainly not a venial sin, and already he can recite the names of the monarchs, in the right order too. 'It would be a waste just to throw away the lollies though,' Margaret-Anne had said. So, every morning, he has handed her the lollies and pocketed the cards. If it wasn't for the little bit of naughtiness she feels, it would be a perfect arrangement. Desmond has lots of cards. He is a collector of all sorts of things. At home in his cupboard he still has last year's Easter egg. He doesn't yet know that his sister has bored a hole in the side and eaten a fragment and discovered it is all white and stale anyway.

'Matti. Matti. Come on. The tram's coming,' Desmond calls to his sister. Everyone at home calls Margaret-Anne Matti. The baptismal name has proved a mistake, such a mouthful. Although the nuns always call her by her full name. 'Such a privilege, Margaret-Anne, to bear two saints' names.'

'Matti. Come on.' Desmond grabs her arm, interrupts her thinking. There is so much to see and think about. Right now she is watching the two Church of England girls. One has plaits. Matti longs for plaits. How do they feel, she wonders. Is it like a monkey's tail? Would it hurt if someone trod on a plait? Matti had curly, golden hair. She wants straight, black, plaited hair. She also wants glasses, crutches and bands on her teeth. How she envies people with broken limbs, especially broken legs, so that as well as the plaster they have a sort of metal bar thing under the foot. Sometimes she winds cotton or rubber bands around her small white teeth in case someone might think she has bands. Once, too, she had kept one eye shut for nearly a week in case glasses might be suggested. 'Stop that at once,' Mummy had finally said. 'Your eyes are perfectly all right. Stop looking for attention.'

'Show-off,' Desmond had said. Sometimes Desmond is awful.

The girl with the plaits and her friend are picking up their cases. Cases. Matti longs for a real Globite case. *Everybody* has Globite cases (and Derwent pencils) except Matti (and Desmond). Mummy says that leather satchels, worn on the back, are far more suitable for the children.

Matti manoeuvres nearer the girls as they ready themselves to step off the kerb and board the tram that is clanging and flashing blue towards them. It is not just the plaits that interest her. First off, they are Church of England girls. Naturally, Matti wouldn't dream of speaking to them. After all, isn't it a mortal sin even to go into one of their churches? Then there is the matter of divorce. Matti knows that there are girls at the Church of England school whose parents are divorced. Divorced! It is one of the most amazing and terrible — and exciting — things she can imagine. Catholics don't get divorced, except one man, 'poor Peter Phillips', who takes the collection plate around at Sunday Mass but can't ever go to Holy Communion again.

All this crams and clutters and sets her brain aflutter. Life is a marvellous adventure of discoveries and maybes and what-ifs. Her whole motion tells of this. Matti rarely walks. She skips or tries tippy-toes or, in moments of great good fun, she might even hop. She is simply quite beautiful to behold.

And why should she be otherwise? Everything is just about perfect in her world. She has Desmond to tell her things. Even before she started school he had taught her history.

'Who crossed the Rubicon?'

'Caesar.'

'Who crossed the Alps?'

'Hannibal.' Lovely, lovely names for what she supposes are great big Harbour Bridge sorts of things. Desmond also has a boy at his school who is a bleeder. 'Like in royal families,' Desmond had told her. Matti is very proud of this. She almost knows a royal person. Desmond is a tremendous help to Matti. And a perfect little gentleman too.

Then there's Mummy and Daddy. Mummy is busy. She has a new baby. Next to Desmond the baby is Matti's favourite thing. Mummy is just Mummy who takes her to Mrs Deutsch, the dressmaker, for viyella dresses and Miss Mueller, the other dressmaker, for seersucker school uniforms. Mummy takes Desmond and Matti to Cahills-with-the-swinging-doors in Castlereagh Street for a treat each holidays. Desmond always has a waffle with caramel sauce and Matti always has chicken sandwiches. Matti always begs Mummy to buy her a peppermint cream in its own special little box but Mummy seldom does so.

Daddy is also busy. Daddy is a doctor. He calls Matti his 'little sheila' and smiles and smiles at her, particularly when she helps Mummy with the baby. Daddy is really a newcomer in Matti's life. He was away at the war, then away studying, and for a long time it was just Mummy and Desmond and Matti at home. Matti still doesn't really know Daddy very well but she has been hearing about him for as long as she can remember. She knows he was a brave soldier. She has seen photos of him in his war clothes. She knows he has had to study very important things so he is very clever. She knows that all this time spent away was for Mummy and Desmond and her. Daddy loves them all very much. He has only been back with them a year and brought such lovely presents and Matti is warm all over when this very important and special person showers his love on her and tells her what a good little sheila she is!

The tram clangs through the bay and up to Point Piper. Desmond gets off. Matti watches him. She wishes she had play lunch in her satchel. Desmond has cake and fruit and a tomato sandwich. Once he had left a banana in his satchel and by the time Mummy found it, it had gone furry and was sort of growing onto the side of the bag. Matti can think of all sorts of lovely things for her lunch but there's no point really. The juniors eat school lunch just like the seniors who are boarders. Mince, mashed potatoes, pumpkin, and sometimes a horrible, exploded apple dumpling with salt lumps.

It is strictly forbidden, a very serious matter, in fact, to bring food to school—except, maybe, cough lollies. Once Matti had brought some black jujubes and pretended Daddy had said she needed them. 'These are for my cough. May I suck them please?' Mother McPhee had given her permission. The other girls usually explained that they had been to the doctor and he had said to suck them. Matti envies them their doctor's visit. She never goes to the doctor. Her own father is a doctor. He never gives out cough lollies. He just pats her on the head and says, 'You'll be all right.' She would like him to give her medicine or take her to a surgery. Mummy says doctors are like that with their own families and, besides, Daddy isn't the sort of doctor who has a surgery. Matti understands that he is something quite a bit more important.

The tram is running along the waterfront. The harbour glistens in the gentle, washy light of early morning. From the promenade edge, long jetties run out into the deep and all manner of craft are moored against them, nosing and bumping like sucklings. The stench of rotten vegetation hits the tram passengers as they pass the narrow inlet where the mud-flats behind the picture theatre are exposed by the low tide, and rank, dark seaweed is alive with skimming water insects. A huge liner hoots mournfully. Red patrol craft are signalling the departure of the great, cumbersome Sunderland flying-boat that is lumbering towards the Heads. Despite the movement and the noise it is tranquil, beautiful.

Matti watches the distant liner. 'Johan van Oldenbarnevelt' she whispers to herself. That was the name of the ship that Daddy had come home on. Such a delicious name. Maybe that's it out there and somewhere, deep down in its bowels, would be the very cabin that Daddy had lived in, all the way from England. The very cabin that she, Matti, had been in, lying on the floor, confused, looking up at the stranger who was hugging Mummy and pointing out a huge, blue box. 'That's for you, little sheila. London Doll's in there for you.'

Wondrous London Doll. So wondrous that she lives in the linen-press in her huge, blue box now and Mummy lets Matti play with her when she goes to the press once a week for clean sheets. London Doll with her sun bonnet and flaxen hair and satin dress and shoes and socks and, best of all, a tiny, weenie teddy in her arms. Matti would love to play with London Doll all the time but Mummy says she is much too good. And that's that.

The tram creeps up the hill and Matti readies herself. There, on the very crest of the hill, is Sacre Coeur. It is a vast, sandstone building, the sandstone softly pink and cream and brown, like coloured ice-cream, the arches and towers and turrets beautifully balanced, though sombre too, and forbidding.

But Matti is lighthearted and confident as she swings down from the tram. For over a year now she has been going to school. She skips though the ornate iron gates, tugs her gloves smooth over her hands, and skirts the Lodge, waving to Mother Portress who sits at the grille. Only visitors go through the Lodge. Down the side path and round the corner she goes, sniffing the lantana. She pauses to peer down into the Grotto where Our Lady's statue is just visible on its lofty, rocky perch. Matti hopes that one day Our Lady might appear to her and tell her secrets, like at Fatima. As she moves on she passes Reverend Mother who is leading the novices on their early morning walk.

She stops and curtseys, as she has been taught, and Reverend Mother inclines her head. Matti watches for a moment as the nuns continue their stroll up and down the lawn. Matti can hardly believe that nuns are people. She pauses again and looks back at them, noticing how their hands are carefully folded out of sight beneath their capes and how their long white veils and frilled bonnets are like blinkers for their eyes so they can't see sideways.

Then Matti resumes her skipping. She rounds the last corner and pushes open the heavy, wooden door. In here is Junior School and it smells familiarly and welcomingly of pencil shavings and shoes and damp. It is the stone walls that smell damp. Matti knows. One day she had pressed her face to their coldness and smelled them.

'Good morning, Margaret-Anne.'

'Good morning, Mother.'

'Run along to Bethlehem, dear, and get ready for Christian Doctrine.'

Matti hurries from her locker in Nazareth to her classroom in Bethlehem. She stops, goes back, collects her gloves which she has put away by mistake in her satchel, pulls them on as required for Christian Doctrine class, tugs at her underpants that are caught in her bottom crack, and starts her day with the Religious of the Sacre Coeur.

Mother McPhee, soft-skinned and dumpy, is Mistress of the Junior School. Thirty-six children and all of them children of God. Mother McPhee considers them her babies, her special gift from a loving Father. She fusses and loves them. They try her and tire her. She fears a motherly inclination to indulge their whims and so, occasionally, to her distress, she is forced to be firm with them.

Mother McPhee is not happy this morning. The little girls are standing behind their chairs, gloves on, waiting for the morning prayer before Christian Doctrine, and, children being children, she knows they won't wait quietly for long. Her face carries an air of distraction. Mairie Molloy's mother has not noticed it. She often pops in for a little chat when she delivers Mairie to school. Years ago she was at school with Mother McPhee — Claire. Once the little girls had actually heard her call Mother McPhee that. It had scarcely seemed believable. They had giggled, shocked, Mairie had been for a short time the centre of attention. The little girls quizzed her: 'Ask your mother. Go on. What colour hair has she got?' Nun's hair, not just Mother McPhee's, is endlessly speculated upon. How terrible to have it all shaved off, forever. It must be dreadful to be a nun and the very worst part would be the hair part.

Mrs Molloy is talking about the Old Girls' Reunion. Mother McPhee's eyes roam the class. The girls are starting to squirm. Matti looks over at Mairie. Does Mairie feel dreadful with her mother here? After all, everyone knows that except on the most special occasions, mothers are not supposed to come into the school. Once the children enter the gates, the nuns become their mothers. Everyone knows that. Except Mairie's mother. Poor Mairie.

Mother McPhee sends up a silent prayer for patience. God has his mysterious ways and Mrs Molloy is having problems in the home. But, heaven's above, it's been going on since last Christmas when the candles burnt down and ignited the brown paper of the Christmas crib while Mrs Molloy was talking and though, thank God, no damage was done, just a mess, the poor woman doesn't seem to realise what an inconvenient time it was, it is, to call.

The five children are not standing up straight any longer. Clack, clack, clack goes the little wooden signal hidden in Mother McPhee's hand. Wordlessly she indicates with her finger that the fidgeting stop. Matti is impatient, bored. She pulls off one glove, leans over and dips her finger in the inkwell in Mother's desk and pops it into her mouth. She turns and faces the glass doors into St Maria Goretti. The kindergarten class see her. She pokes out her tongue and waggles it. The babies start to giggle and point. Mother Freeman, who has no parent distracting her, looks up and sees Matti. She moves swiftly.

'Mother McPhee, Margaret-Anne is distracting the children.' Mother McPhee puts a restraining arm on Mrs Molloy, excuses herself firmly and stands before Matti. Matti does not like the musty anonymous smell of the black serge habit. She averts her head.

'Look at me, please, dear,' says Mother McPhee. 'What have you got in your mouth?'

'Nothing, Mother,' says Matti boldly.

'Open your mouth.' Matti opens her mouth. 'Tongue out, please. That is a very short tongue. Right out, please.' Matti doesn't feel quite so daring anymore. She extends her blue-black, rusty-tasting tongue.

'Go to my room, Margaret-Anne. Wait for me there. I am very disappointed in you.'

Matti goes, sorry now. She likes her lessons and, probably, she will have to remain in Mother's office until lunch time. Poo. And she likes Mother McPhee. She's really like another mother. She loves Matti. Matti knows that very surely. Poo. She passes the empty room with the huge, old-fashioned dentist's chair where the nuns see the visiting dentist, and enters Mother McPhee's office. She sits down on the carved monk's bench against the wall and stares gloomily at the shadows.

Reverend Mother is on her way to visit the juniors. Who is this she catches sight of in Mother McPhee's office? Reverend Mother has never taught little girls. Her talents lie elsewhere. The little ones are God's angels on earth. So, she takes Matti's hand and leads her back to the classroom. The class rise in unison. 'Good morning, Reverend Mother,' they chant. They all curtsey.

'Excuse me, Mother McPhee,' says Reverend Mother courteously. 'I am sure Margaret-Anne meant no harm. Perhaps it was an accident.' Mother McPhee inclines her head deferentially. One does not disagree with Reverend Mother, although one may feel the sin of irritation pricking.

'I'm sure Margaret-Anne will make a lovely St Tarsisius.' Mother McPhee cannot prevent her eyes widening in surprise.

'Yes, Reverend Mother. But we did decide on one or other of the twinnies.'

'Yes, Mother McPhee, we did. But that was what I was coming to tell you. Their dear mother rang me this morning. The twinnies have the mumps. Margaret-Anne will be our St Tarsisius.'

Like any mother, Mother McPhee finds herself drawn more easily to some children than to others. Mother McPhee is a human being under the habit. She battles these natural inclinations and is scrupulously fair and left to herself she would not have chosen Matti, for Matti is someone she is drawn to and choosing her after this morning's episode would be unfair. Still, Reverend Mother has spoken. Mother McPhee might live the life of an enclosed religious but that does not make her unworldly. She believes that life is hard and only firmness and discipline will prepare her charges for life. Matti must learn that being chosen for special privileges brings with its special responsibilities. She must learn that it is Our Blessed Lord who has bestowed gifts on her and, therefore, much will be required of her. She must learn, and learn early, that she owes it, constantly owes it, to God, her parents and her teachers, to strive for perfection in thanks for these gifts.

Therefore, Mother McPhee takes Matti aside that afternoon and speaks firmly to her.

'Margaret-Anne, you have disappointed me very much with your silly behaviour. Both Reverend Mother and I are concerned at your lack of discipline. Reverend Mother, in her wisdom, has decided that St Tarsisius will be a great help to you. You will have to be a very good girl. It would be sinful to misbehave when you have been entrusted with such a great honour.'

'Oh, I promise, Mother. I promise. I will be good. I promise. Thank you, Mother. I'm sorry, Mother.'

'Very well, dear. I hope so. Remember, this is a very great privilege. Run along now.' She taps the child gently on the head. She longs to hold a child in her arms and hug and hug. Her heart yearns. She must pray that God, in His divine wisdom, will fill this vacuum.

Sometimes Matti is a bit naughty at home too.

Matti is riding on Aunty Ely's back. She is forbidden to ride on Aunty Ely's back. Now Mummy has come in and spoken sharply and Matti has slid down onto the floor that Aunty Ely is scrubbing.

'Matti, how many times have I told you that you are not to do that? Aunty Ely has a bad back.' (Which Matti knows. Don't they pray, every night, in their night prayers, for God to make Aunty Ely's back better, and Uncle Harold's nose and Mrs Demerald's chest?) 'If you do that again, you will get the wooden spoon.' Matti looks in alarm at Aunty Ely, who smiles at her. Who loves her. Aunty Ely wouldn't let her get the wooden spoon. She puts her arms around the kneeling woman's neck and squeezes her hard and kisses all over her face. Oh, that lovely damp feel on Aunty Ely's face. That soft, soft skin.

Matti sometimes thinks that she would like Aunty Ely to be her mother. Aunty Ely has never been cross with her. Except when Matti climbs onto her back, and even then, well, you could hardly call it cross. She just says that Matti is making Baby Jesus sad and if Matti is a good girl there will be yet another diamond in the lovely crown that is being prepared for her up in heaven. Matti can see that crown. She loves it, knowing it is waiting up there for her, all sparkly and with lots of tinsel like the one the fairy queen wore in the pantomime that Mummy took her and Desmond to.

Matti decides she will be a good girl and help wash the floor and Aunty Ely gives her a little rag and the two of them work together. Aunty Ely is a wonderful and mysterious person. Her first name is Gypsy. Imagine! Gypsy Ely. Coloured scarves, gold medallions, crystal balls, fortune-telling. Matti read all about gypsies in a book Daddy brought back from England.

'Don't be silly, Matti,' says Mummy. 'Of course Aunty Ely is not a gypsy.'

'But that's her name.'

'Aunty Ely is a pillar of St Francis' up at Paddington,' says Mummy. Matti can't make much sense of it. It is the most wonderful name she has ever heard. And Aunty Ely is the most wonderful person. She is fat, fat, fat. When she hugs Matti, and she and Matti are always hugging, she is spongy and soft and, at the top of her dress, it's all crinkly skin and a hanky tucked away down there in the crack. And Aunty Ely smells so good. Damp, cool.

And this afternoon when Aunty Ely has finished her housework for Mrs Milton she and Matti are going to her house. Matti is sometimes allowed to do that, to 'help' Aunty Ely. They cross the green lawn and cool grassy spaces into the treeless suburb with old boarded-up terraces and the children playing in the street. Matti grips Aunty Ely's hand tight as they pass the hotel. Matti is terrified of hotels, the noise and the smell and all the Horrible Old Creatures, as Mummy calls them. Now they enter Aunty Ely's street and she says hullo nicely to all the people that Aunty Ely tells her to. Aunty Ely seems to know so many people. More than

Mummy and Daddy anyway. Now they enter the house. Matti knows that she mustn't go into the front room. No-one ever does. It must be kept just so in case the parish priest drops in. Also she must not go upstairs. Aunty Ely has boarders and they mustn't be disturbed. But she can go into the kitchen and into Aunty Ely's bedroom. Which is what she does. Always does. It is so wonderful with the picture. 'Tell me about it again, Aunty Ely.'

'That is St Veronica. She wiped the face of Jesus — Matti, don't forget to bow your head when you hear the name of Jesus — when He was carrying His cross to Calvary. So that's her and she's showing you the cloth. See?'

'And I can see Jesus' face on it. I can. And His eyes follow me, don't they? Wherever I am in your room, they follow me. It's magic. It's magic.'

'No, Matti. It's a miracle.'

'A miracle. A miracle.' Matti spends a lot of time in this room, trying to trick the picture. Spinning around suddenly. Peeping. Trying to catch it unawares. Aunty Ely is right. It is a miracle.

'Oh, Aunty Ely. Guess what? I'm in the play. At school. I'm St Tarsisius.'

'Are you, darling? Well, isn't that lovely. God bless you. Now you'll be a very good girl, won't you, with such a special privilege?' Matti nods her head.

'Of course, I will. Mother McPhee told me already.'

The weeks of rehearsals for the Death of St Tarsisius occupy the Junior School and Matti wonders how life could ever have seemed even a bit exciting before. She loves it all. Especially she loves the short, white, silky tunic that she wears, bound at her waist with a gold, tasselled cord. About her hair, Mother McPhee binds a leather thong. One morning when Reverend Mother pops in to hand out lollies and holy cards and check the play's progress, Matti hears her whisper, 'angelic'.

As St Tarsisius Matti has to hurry through the streets of Rome, protecting the Blessed Sacrament, which she carries in the bodice of her tunic, from the assaults and outrages of any pagan Romans who happen by. The other juniors are the pagan throng. They must set upon her and attempt to tear away the precious burden. Matti must resist and call upon Divine Intervention until she falls to the ground—and death. How she twists and ducks, grimaces and doubles up, falls and twitches and squirms.

'Margaret-Anne. Don't wave your legs about like that, please. Try to be a little more lady-like.' Matti lies motionless, feeling dead, heroic, wonderful. 'Margaret-Anne, do get up at once from the lino before you catch a chill,' orders Mother McPhee.

Later in the same year the months of preparation begin for the splendour of First Holy Communion. Matti's classmates are the privileged ones of the Junior School. Patiently, month after month, Mother McPhee teaches them the significance of the approaching day. She shows them special holy cards and takes them in the Junior School parlour for Congregation, where they are given secret intentions to pray for, little penances of self-denial to perform and spiritual reading to read.

Mother Lacey, a novice in a white veil, supervises a group of juniors while Mother McPhee conducts Friday afternoon Congregation. Mother Lacey has no experience of children and dreads Friday afternoons. The children seem particularly silly and rude on Fridays.

'Sit down. I . . . no, not now, Anne. Well, if you must. Put away your skipping rope, Elizabeth, and sit down. Are we all . . . No, not now. Yes, Marella?'

'Please, Mother. Can we have our own Mongregation?'

'Whatever do you mean?'

'Mongregation. You know. Like them. You tell us secrets and things, and things to do and . . .'

'Don't be silly, dear. Sit down now and when you are a First Communicant your turn will come.'

'But . . .'

'Sit down!' Mother Lacey is alarmed by the shrill pitch in her voice. She wonders whether she likes little girls very much. They are all so . . . so smarty-pants. Oh, and look at that awful Noni Plowman just sitting there, face like a log, knitting with that frightful purple wool on needles like fence posts. Fence posts . . . Mother Lacey smiles. Less than twelve months ago she had been riding round, checking fence posts with Dad at home up at Walgett.

'If you sit very still and are nice and quiet, I'll tell you about my horse,' she says. The class sit up. A nun with a horse? Mother Lacey closes the story book and starts to talk.

In the parlour Congregation continues. The little girls are excited about the approaching day and listen, uncomprehendingly, as Mother Porter explains the Sacred Mysteries. Matti can't imagine that the really-truly Jesus will come into her at Communion, but she's prepared to believe it. That's called faith, says Mother McPhee.

What concerns and interests the group are other, more specific matters. Mother McPhee explains. 'If you commit a mortal sin and go to Communion without first having the forgiveness from a true Confession, then you have committed a double mortal sin and you will go straight to hell.'

'If you died,' clarifies Matti.

'Naturally,' says Mother McPhee who tries hard to stress to her disciples that it is practically impossible for them to commit a mortal sin at their age.

'But what if you kill someone?' asks Matti.

'I hardly think you are going to kill anyone, dear,' says Mother McPhee.

The matters of sin and punishment and Confession continue, however, to occupy Matti's thoughts. Never mind a mortal sin, she can never think up enough ordinary old venial sins for Friday Confession and wonders if Father Bates thinks she is, perhaps, keeping something back. 'Three Hail Marys, God bless you, my child,' is all he ever says. Sometimes Matti thinks he may have dropped off to sleep behind the ornately carved, wooden grille, as there are long silences between their utterances. But, no. With a painful intake of breath, the old priest groans into life. 'Oh, my God, I am heartily sorry...' and Matti takes up the prayer of absolution. Gradually she becomes accustomed to his demeanour and decides her sins are quite presentable enough and her weekly encounter becomes as comfortable and predictable as Mother McPhee's moony morning face.

Tomorrow is the great day and the group are reminded that they must take no food or drink after midnight.

'You may, if you are ill, take a sip of water. But only if absolutely necessary,' says Mother McPhee.

Matti approaches her First Communion with great excitement and gladness of heart. On this special day their parents are welcomed inside the convent, one of the few occasions when home and school overlap, and all the more significant because of that. Matti's class assembles early, with their parents, in Reverend Mother's parlour. Desmond has come too, but has been led to the sacristy to be issued with his altar-boy clothes.

Shyly and silently (for silence is enjoined upon them before Communion), the classmates sneak glances at each other's white dresses and shoes and filmy gloves. Matti is just the tiniest bit disappointed with her dress. Mummy has had it made by Mrs Deutsch, not liking the ready-made offerings in the religious stores. It is voile and exquisitely pin-tucked and very plain. Matti had hoped there might be frills and petticoats.

Reverend Mother and her helpers arrive with the French veils and wreaths, heirlooms from the Mother House in France. The veiling is ceremonial and stately. Each small child stands between her parents, the great wreath low on her brow, waiting to be led to the chapel.

Now the glory begins. Reverend Mother ushers them away from their parents to the doors of the great Gothic chapel. Here they wait, solemn and filled with awe, for the signal to move up the aisle. The arched, sandstone roof soars up before them, and their goal, the threshold of the huge marble altar, seems remote and splendid. It is ablaze with candles, and white and yellow flowers burst from their vases in an orgy of dizzying profusion. In the wooden stalls around the chapel walls the choir nuns are finishing Morning Office, sing-song chanting, invocation and response echoing through the rafters. In the pews in the body of the chapel, the boarders kneel motionless. On no account are they permitted to sit or to turn around for a better view of the communicants.

The Office ends and the chapel waits, hushed. From the organ gallery drop notes of sweet purity and the communicants start their long, solemn walk up the aisle. When they reach the altar rails they spread out and move, rehearsed to perfection, to the prie-dieus which await them, covered in white satin and bound with white ribbons and flowers. Behind each is a padded, satin-covered stool. Matti supposes that this is what heaven is like. She kneels, heady and dreamy, dazzled by the scents, the music, the creamy, flickering candles, hundreds and hundreds of them.

The rubrics of the liturgy proceed about her.

Then the organ peals forth in triumph. Matti and the little band of communicants leave the chapel reverently and walk into the waiting embraces of Reverend Mother and the community. Matti is passed from nun to nun, feeling their lips brush her cheek and hearing their frilly bonnets make a crackly sound against her ear. Then the holy cards and special rosary beads are handed out and the children move with their parents to the dining room where the nuns wait to serve the celebratory breakfast.

This morning is truly important to them all. They are the centre of attention. It is all praise and exclamation, blessings and en-chantment, and photos with the Box Brownie.

But, a year later, there is another batch of communicants. Matti has to observe it all, regretfully, enviously, from the pews. Miracles and magic have passed.

FOUR

Mrs Milton is at home, stripping the four-poster bed. Her breath comes in wheezy gasps. Her nose drips. There is something, heaven knows what, about the bed that brings on her wheezes and drips. She sighs as she casts the bottom sheet, skilfully as a fisherman, across the mattress. Her belly is cumbersome and her veins throb and she would like to fall across the bed, face first, and lie motionless forever. But, no. There is so much to be done, and first, this bed. She is resigned to the morning bed-making ritual now, although when her husband first returned she had been surprised and resentful.

'I will not tolerate a slovenly bed,' he had said. 'Beds are to be completely stripped, the mattress turned daily and the bedding aired before re-making.'

'But Patrick, surely twice a... Oh, very well.' She had seen his face, a face she did not remember from before. She had seen the coldness creep into his eyes and had been puzzled, afraid even.

Mrs Milton leans across to smooth the sheet. She pulls tightly at the corner and executes a neat nurse's corner. She straightens her back, pressing with her hand on the troublesome sciatic nerve, and sniffs loudly. She fishes in her apron pocket and pulls out her sodden hanky and swabs her wet nose. She fishes again and brings out a mint jujube. She pops it into her mouth and feels calmer. Mint jujubes are her little secret.

Oh dear, so much to do, and do thoroughly. The stranger who returned to her from England has attitudes which have well-nigh overwhelmed her. She lives on a parade ground. As she walks to the chair to collect the pillows she glances in the mirror and looks quickly away from the drab with the dark shadowed eyes who stares back at her. Is this the same woman who dressed up in a crinoline and won the Scarlett O'Hara prize? The woman in a top hat and tails, dancing down a table at the Trocadero? Surely not!

'Yes it is, it is,' she whispers, glaring at the woman in the mirror. 'I wasn't always like this. I don't even know how it happened. How did it happen?' Oh, fatal question. Mrs Milton starts to cry, snuffling miserably, drip, drip, drip. Heavens above! She is sitting on the freshly-made bed.

But why is it such a surprise to her? He had warned her often enough, had he not, in the letters from England. Letters about no longer burning the candle at both ends. Letters about the seriousness of life and the need to get on and the sacrifices this would entail. Now she knows what it all means. He will work and life will be rigorous and she will be the stalwart support, providing every ounce of her being to care for him and the big family that is ordained.

Mrs Milton blows her nose decisively. 'Well, this won't buy the child a dress.' In irritation she tries to re-adjust the bulging belly that hampers her every move. 'Marriage is sacrifice,' says her husband, Patrick, 'and give and take.' She walks briskly out to collect the carpet-sweeper. Plenty of take. Where's all the give? No, that is unfair. He works hard. It's for us all. Is it? She resolves to push away these thoughts. She will try harder. He will be pleased—and it will keep the peace.

Keep the peace. Harder and harder. Desmond and Matti for one thing. No longer infants. No longer angels. So hard to know what to do. Why won't they play together like they used to? They should. They must. A family is complete unto itself, states Dr Milton. Desmond and Matti must learn to get on together again and stop this constant whine that they be allowed out the front gate to join the trikes and scooters that rattle up and down every afternoon after school. Mummy has explained and explained to them that Daddy says playing on the footpath (and going barefoot) is rough. 'One thing leads to another. Next thing it will be the pool hall,' he says. Which Mummy secretly doubts. But, there it is.

Desmond and Matti are impossibly quarrelsome. As Mrs Milton

goes about her morning tasks, the two children crouch beside the back steps.

'No, you're the customer.'

'No, you are.'

'No, I'm the butcher.'

'It's not fair. You're always the butcher.'

'Well, I'm a boy, stupid,' says Desmond, expertly chopping the hibiscus buds into lumps of meat. 'You have to go away and come back in a minute and ask me to make up a meat order for you.'

Matti trots up the path and sits under the letter box, waiting for Desmond to be ready. She adjusts her hat and organises her basket on her arm. When Desmond calls she will slip her feet into Mummy's old high heel shoes.

'Open. Ready,' yodels her brother. Matti takes a moment to fit her sandalled feet into the shoes and totters down the path to the butcher shop.

'Good morning, Mrs Magerkinshaw,' says Desmond.

'Good morning, Mr Mainsbridge,' says Matti, all high and sing-songy.

'Isn't it awful about poor Lily Maxwell?'

'Oh? I hadn't heard.'

'She fell off the tram,' giggles Matti, 'on her way into town to Mr Stegmar for a perm and . . .'

'That's enough. Come on, Matti. Order the meat.' Desmond waves the knife.

'Oh, very well.' Hoity-toity. 'I'd like six chump chops and a leg of lamb, please.'

'No, you have to order only one thing at a time, so I don't run out.'

'But I'll bring it back,' says Matti. Desmond looks crafty.

'You can't bring it back. You know the rules. Whoever is the customer has to eat the meat.'

'Well, I'm not playing then. I hate you. And I'll tell Mummy you took the knife.'

'Come on Matti. That's the rule. You've ordered six chump chops. You have to eat them.'

'I won't.'

'Well, I'll let you off then but you have to eat the leg of lamb.'

'I won't.'

'You have to. It's the rules we made up.'

Matti tears off her hat and kicks off her shoes. 'I won't eat that horrible thing. Mummy said I was never to eat another one.' The hibiscus lies meaty and slimy on the step.

'Spoil-sport. Tittle-tat. You've got to eat it or I'll never play with you again. Never.' He starts to walk away. Matti looks frantically at the meat. It is so boring with no one to play with.

'Desmond. Please. I'll do anything else you ask but not the meat. I'll vomit. Please stay and play. I'll do whatever you say. Please.'

'Promise?' asks Desmond.

'Promise.'

'Cross your heart and spit to death and hope to die?'

'Yes. Cross my heart and spit to death and hope to die.'

Desmond ambles back to the arena. 'Clean up the butcher's shop first,' he commands. Gratefully she tips the rotten old flowers into the garden. 'Now come down the back and I'm going to make you put your finger in Tom's hole.' Matti gasps. Desmond's game! The Tom game! The horrible monster person who lives in the dark behind the cobwebs that cover the hole in the bricks. The monster who kills little children, especially little girls by biting their fingers with poisonous teeth. After the smacks last week he said he'd never do the Tom game again!

'No, Desmond. You're not allowed.'

'You swore, Matti.' Yes, she did.

Sick with fear she follows Desmond round the back. He pushes aside the leaves of the *Monstera deliciosa* and opens a small door behind it, set low in the sandstone foundations. He pushes her through and follows. They crouch breathless in the dark and the dank.

'Tom,' calls Desmond. 'Tom. Wake up. Matti's here to see you. She's going to put her finger in your hole. Tom. Tom.' His voice is soft.

'No, please no, Desmond. Don't call him. Don't make that singy sound. I'll do it. I promise. If you stop that calling.'

'No sticking it in then running away?'

'No. I promise.'

'All right. Come over here.' He takes her arm and pulls her against the stone. Between the slabs is a black, cobwebby hole. 'Put it in. Go on.'

'Let go of me first.' Desmond lets go. Quick as a flash Matti heads for the door. Desmond is there before her.

'You liar, Matti. You little cheat. You promised. Now I'm going to have to make you.'

'No, Desmond. No.' Matti begins to yell. Desmond pulls her back to the hole, wrestles her hand into submission and plunges her finger into the hole. Matti howls in terror. Wee, hot and pungent, runs down her legs.

'You pig, Matti. You've wet your pants.' Desmond punches Matti in the back and runs to the door. 'Pig,' he repeats as he runs through, slams it behind him and races away.

In the darkness, locked in, Matti continues to scream. She screams in fury and fear and shame. She screams in hatred of her brother. And finally, when she is nearly exhausted, Mummy comes and pulls her crossly out and whips off her smelly wet underpants and tells her she is a very silly little girl to play those silly games with Desmond.

'But he made me.'

'Don't be silly, Matti. Go and tidy up your dollies and keep away from him. Daddy can deal with him tonight.'

They keep a sullen distance from each other for the remainder of the day. Matti helps Mummy do the lamingtons, coating each cut square in chocolate and rolling it in coconut. She is occupied yet eager for a playmate. But Desmond sulks. Desmond can be a very sulky boy.

Now it is nearly time. The time when he comes. At Mummy's urging, all signs of toys and games are packed neatly away and Matti is sent to check the path is clear of trikes. Mummy hurries upstairs to freshen her lipstick and take off her apron and change her frock. Daddy likes order and neatness when he comes home after a hard day. It is the least he can expect. Otherwise words will be spoken.

He has come and greeted them and Mummy, oh dear, has told on them. Mummy, quite frankly, doesn't know how to cope with Desmond and Matti when they quarrel. She is inclined to hold

Matti responsible. If Matti didn't make such a fuss... Desmond is summoned. His misdemeanours are spelled out to him.

'What have you got to say for yourself, son?' asks Daddy. Desmond says nothing, staring at a spot somewhere to the left of Daddy's head.

'Speak up!' Nothing. 'Very well. You leave me no choice. Fetch the wooden spoon.'

Matti's tummy takes a big breath. She knows the ritual by heart. The slow march to the kitchen, the rattling about in the second drawer, the march back, the handing over of the implement, the order for palm or pants down. The feinting, the dodging, the barked order, the crack of wood on flesh, the intake of breath, the ritual of accepting back the weapon. 'Thank you, Daddy,' and replacing it in the drawer. Then the apology.

But tonight, Desmond is bold. What is this? No wooden spoon? Yes, Desmond has snapped it in two and thrown it down the storm-water drain. Matti's eyes flash in alarm between her mother and her father and her brother. She wonders if she should have screamed down at Tom's hole. Was it that bad? There's trouble here.

'Bring me the medical journal,' says Daddy. Seemingly indifferent, Desmond does so. Now he must lower his pants and the journal is applied to his buttocks. Harshly, sternly, in sorrow. Matti flinches with each of the eight strokes. Desmond straightens up, pale and grim. 'Let that be the last time I am forced to deal with your bullying ways, son. You are forbidden to hurt your sister. You are forbidden ever to strike a girl. Do I make myself clear?'

'Yes.'

'Yes, what?'

'Yes. Thank you.'

'All right, old man. Let's shake hands and make friends. Your old Dad hates to hit you. Friends?' Doctor Milton proffers his hand but the boy has turned defiantly away. The doctor sets his lips grimly. His face drains of colour. He is not accustomed to defiance. He will not be defied. 'Stand behind the door, Desmond. When you are prepared to apologise and accept your punishment like a man, you may join us at the table.'

What a wretched meal. Knives and forks rattle forlornly. Mrs Milton looks at the door and from time to time looks angrily at

Matti. Matti's heart pounds. She is guilty and penitent. Finally Mrs Milton breaks the silence.

'His dinner's getting cold, Patrick.'

'Naturally. But Desmond knows what he has to do if he wishes to eat a hot meal.'

'But it will be spoilt.'

'Very well, my dear. Matti, take Desmond's dinner and put it in the refrigerator.' Mrs Milton finds this hard to believe. 'In the refrigerator please Matti. He may eat it cold but unspoiled.' Matti rises and looks towards her mother for guidance. 'Hurry up,' barks her father. Matti moves around the table and picks up the plate. Her mother looks away in disgust. She passes the door. Judas. Judas.

Desmond will not apologise. In fury, Dr Milton sends him out into the darkness, down near Tom's hole, to chop kindling. Crack, crack, crack. As she lies in her warm bed, Matti hears the distant blows as the tomahawk splinters the wood.

For days the house is tense. Desmond will not apologise. Doctor Milton will not speak. Mummy buys Desmond a Hornby train. She talks urgently to him in his room. Is that the hint of a smile that Matti sees on his face as he says, 'Sorry, Daddy'? Is that the swagger of a winner?

Matti is subdued. She has been watching Daddy. She has been afraid of the grim set of his lips. She has missed the way he ruffles her curls. He has not really been Daddy at all. She has thought, has felt, how terrible it would be to be out there in the dark. It must never happen to her. She will always do what Daddy says and she will be safe. How will she please him so that he never puts her out? She will help Mummy. That's what she will do. Daddy is always pleased when she is helpful. Oh, Desmond, you are silly sometimes. Don't you see how easy it is to please Daddy?

FIVE

Matti pleases Daddy by helping Mummy with the babies. Desmond and Matti are the big ones. Daddy is 'inculcating the disciplines'. There are also by now three new little chaps. Here she goes, hurrying up the stairs with the heated vegetables, the bottle in hot water, the sterile teat turned down into the bottle. See how competently she places these on the chest of drawers and scoops the sodden, smelly baby boy from the bassinet.

'You're getting too big for this bed,' she scolds. 'You'll have to go into the cot when Mummy has a new baby. You'll like the cot, won't you, darling?' She buries her nose in the fold of fat on his tummy and blows farty little bubbles onto his skin. The baby squeals with delight and clamps his fists around Matti's curls and pulls.

'Ow! Let go.' Gently, always gently, she disentangles herself and prepares him for his bath. His eyes follow her every move as she tests the water with her crooked elbow, lays out the soap and the towels and the fresh clothes for after. Matti is efficient in the nursery and happy. So happy. Her little brothers smile and cling to her. She is loved and needed and wanted and above all, Daddy is pleased that she is so helpful. She sings a little song, so happy does she feel this sunny morning. Daddy is passing the nursery.

'You sound like a worn-out record, Matti. For heaven's sake, try and hit the note. You'd terrify tigers with that noise.' Matti flushes with shame and falls silent. She hears her mother speaking.

'Don't be saying that to her, Patrick. You'll put her off. It's nice to hear her singing.'

'Well, she hasn't got the ear, my dear. You either have it or you

40

haven't and poor old Matti hasn't and there it is.' Matti hears him laugh as he moves away. Her face feels flushed. She trembles.

'Don't take any notice of him,' says her mother, coming in and seeing that she had heard. *Don't take any notice?* Doesn't she know that Matti always takes notice of Daddy? She's his little sheila.

Each year Daddy and Desmond and Matti take their journey together. Just the three of them, having an adventure, but an adventure that is all the more wonderful because its progress can be charted by how it was done last year and the year before and . . .

It is Boxing Day when they leave and it is hot and four a.m.

'Must you leave so early?' says Mummy.

'I want to beat the traffic,' says Daddy. But the road to the Hawkesbury is already jammed with cars and Matti squirms a bit because once, on this winding road she vomited all over her colouring book with the blue and the yellow budgerigars. But after the Hawkesbury bridge everyone perks up because no-one has ever been sick from here on. And a litany of remembered habits. 'We always do our wees here' and 'this is where we get the milkshakes and toasted sandwiches' and 'my turn in the front'.

Matti wins the cherry sucking competition, with a cherry in her mouth all the way from Hexham to Aberdeen. And in the late afternoon they stop beside the tumbledown shack that Daddy calls 'the kids' cubby'. (And 'kids' a forbidden word too!) There Daddy combs their hair and smooths out Matti's dress and they know that very soon the little town at the foot of the Moonbi ranges, the lovely blue Moonbis, will come into view and there they will stay for a while.

Matti curls her body in anticipation as they approach. She will see her grandmother who is tiny and never cranky and has a bun. Already she can feel the hugs of the small woman and smell the house. She can smell the heavy druggy scent of violets down the side passage and the over-ripe smell of fallen valencias that carpet an entire lawn, and the foul pungent odour of the thrips on the roses. She can smell the citronella and the waxy night light that burns before the Infant of Prague and the Little Flower.

Matti can see already the strange old mother-of-pearl inlay cabinets that dot the house, and the hat-stand with ancient hats and walking sticks and old golf balls in drawers and postcards and brown, curling photographs and draped, crocheted afghans.

Matti can hear the burn and roar of the black chip-heater that spews scalding water into the claw-footed tub and see the bottle on the washstand labelled Solyptol. 'Solly pottle, solly pottle, solly pottle,' she whispers to herself. And the translucent ovals of Pears soap that glow like amber.

Matti dreams. She dreams enchanted dreams of her grandmother. Maybe her grandmother will wash her hair while they are there. The mysterious bun that they love to prod will be unwound before their spellbound eyes, the large hair pins laid in the silver-lidded glass jar, the cloud of thick, white hair brushed into a halo. Then out onto the back lawn they will go, with the kitchen chair and the tin basins and then the little lady will wash it and it will be all lemony-tang. Matti thrills in anticipation. Their grandmother, carefree as a girl, scrubbing, dunking, dousing, then her hair drying magnificently about her shoulders.

And so it is, just as Matti pictured.

Then they move on. Another journey. Another grandparent. Again the early start in the cool of the day, with a huge cardboard box of sandwiches—curried egg, chook, banana—all firmly padded with lettuce leaves, packed in greaseproof paper, and slabs of Aunty Someone's fruitcake. More miles, more quizzes, more backseat wrestling with Desmond. More diversions. Thunderbolt and Uralla, Bluff Rock, and a visit to the cathedral at Armidale. On and on, to the Stanthorpe border and triumphantly in to Brisbane.

And it is triumphant. The little girl twitches with delight as she stands with her head sticking through the sunroof of the old car as they trundle over the Story Bridge and through the Valley to the huge house where the grandfather lives.

Nights of mosquito nets and heavy heat and mornings where breakfast is formal and adult. Days of bachelor uncles who will let Matti and Desmond drive the car, and fish, and puff cigarettes, and maybe take them to the gasworks at Pinkenba for a picnic. And wonderful stories of the Red Admiral and Dick Whittington and police and drunken witches. Days of tropical colour, bougainvillea, poinciana, mangoes, pawpaws, and a grandfather who likes a good alarming argument at meals. Matti frisks around, remembering her manners, seeing Daddy smile proudly when she speaks up nicely and remembers to say 'thank you for having me' when they leave for home.

It is late and Matti is tired. Daddy is 'putting his foot down' and they're driving through the night for home. The spell has been broken. Going home is quite a different thing from going away. Many miles and few towns in between. The bush is black and lonely. Desmond is lying down across the back seat. Matti is sitting in the front with Daddy. Her eyes sting with tiredness and her head nods forward, jerking her awake every few minutes. She decides to stop helping Daddy drive and snuggle down and go to sleep, like every year.

She wiggles her feet up under her bottom and leans across the handbrake and cushions herself comfortably, safely, warmly, in Daddy's lap. Like always.

'Matti! Sit up at once.' He jerks her shoulder, her head is wrenched aside. 'Sit up!'

'I'm tired, Daddy. I want to go to sleep.'

'You're much too big for that, Matti. Sit up at once.' She pulls away. Sits up. Blotches of red, wild things sing in her head. She rubs her eyes.

'Please . . .' The car slews to the dirt.

'Hop in the back, Matti. Desmond, come on, son. In the front.'

She crawls into the back, stretches across the hard seat. It is dark and lonely all the way from him. Her hand slips into the comforting warmness between her thighs. She longs for the warm Daddy-smell of him.

One of Matti's favourite things in the whole house is Mummy and Daddy's bed. Matti has never seen a bed like it except in a book of fairy tales. She has told her school friends about it but none of them has ever seen such a bed. (Perhaps one day she can bring them home to see the bed? Maybe not, because Daddy says she has her brothers to play with and that is enough. He does not approve of children visiting strange homes. No birthday parties, no serials, no *Women's Weekly*. It's all for their own good.)

The bed is an olden-days bed with four tall carved wooden posts and a frill around the top. The posts have carved roses and tulips and tendrils of ivy and Matti loves to trace them with her finger. Just touching them makes her believe she is part of a fairy tale. At the foot of each post is a smooth rectangular panel and one of these panels is hinged so that if you press it and push it upwards at the same time it slips out of its hinge and comes loose. Inside is a cavity that could be used for all sorts of things. Matti can't understand why no-one uses it here. You could hide secret letters or a map or jewels... anything... 'Stop romancing, Matti,' says Mummy when Matti asks her why she doesn't hide anything inside the panel. 'You're a great little romancer.' Matti still hopes that having told them how useful and secret it is, they might be prompted to use it. She checks regularly.

And the bed itself. Another of Matti's favourite things is sharing it with Mummy and Daddy. Creeping in in the early morning and watching Mummy feed the baby his bottle. Matti knows that once she had been fed like this and once too she would have been the next youngest and little enough to snuggle in between Mummy and Daddy. She understands this natural progression and curls contentedly at the foot of the bed, waiting for her chance to have a morning cuddle of the baby and take him back to his nursery on the verandah.

There are special occasions when she does have a go, a proper go, in the big bed. If Daddy has to go away, or Mummy, less often, they are allowed to take turns sleeping there. Now Mummy has gone away for a day or so and it is Matti's turn in the big bed. She is excited. She has even used Mummy and Daddy's bathroom because you are allowed to when you are sleeping in the big bed. She had pulled on her pyjamas and jumped into Mummy's side of the bed and... what's this? Daddy has come in and he is angry. So angry

'What do you think you're doing?'

'It's my turn.'

'Get out of there at once, Matti.'

'But it's my turn.'

'You heard me. At once. Go and tell Desmond to come in. He's to sleep here tonight...'

'But it's my turn.'

'You are to go to your room at once. I absolutely forbid it. You are not to sleep in here again. Is that clear?' Matti scrambles from the bed. For some reason that she cannot understand she feels afraid, and bad, as if she has done some monstrous thing. She does not understand what this can be. She crawls into her own bed and pulls the covers up over her head. Her special place has been taken away from her. All she wants is to please Daddy and be close to him.

She will be uneasy now near the great bed. She will open the secret panel hardly at all. Rarely will she join that group all atumble in the morning bedclothes. She must not. There is something dangerous and bad there and she may stumble on it unawares. But what? What?

Dr and Mrs Milton lie side by side in the marital bed. The marital duty is done. She can at least be grateful for that. He is warmly expansive. He strokes her tired face. He loves her.

'There is a little matter I would like to make clear, my dear. Desmond and Matti are growing up.' He raises his hand authoritatively. 'They are not getting the discipline they need. Desmond I am less worried about. A firm hand is all he needs. He is a credit to us. The good Fathers are delighted with his progress. But Matti is something else altogether. Matti will be a wife and mother some day, please God. She must learn, early on, that life is tough. As you well know. And with that in mind, I must be allowed my way. Matti needs discipline.' Mrs Milton lies passively and hears it all. She wonders why he tells her. Doesn't he always do what he thinks best? She is tired. Worn out. One day her daughter will know this same exhaustion. There's no escaping it. She could sleep for a hundred years. What new difficulty is he throwing at her now?

Dr Milton has thought through very carefully the whole matter of early morning swimming lessons. He is deeply committed to the belief that fresh air and exercise are highly beneficial in any number of unspecified physical and mental areas but most especially discipline. Sport builds character and as Matti will not have the benefit of a good game of rugger later on, it is all the more important that she take her swimming lessons to heart. Years ago when he first came back he had tried to teach Desmond and Matti boxing. Didn't he buy boxing gloves and teach them the rudiments of the game? On the principle that you have to be able to take a knock or two. Was it his fault if it was premature?

'Come on. Come on,' he had urged, twisting and weaving above them, down on his knees for accessibility. 'Come on, put your hearts into it. Come on, Matti. Hit me. Hit me.' No, it had not been a success. The children would not hit their father. But time has elapsed. The boxing had possibly been an error of judgement, but in the matter of the swimming there is no mistake. Didn't he go early morning swimming summer and winter when he was a boy? It didn't hurt him, did it? It's tough, yes. But character building. He begins.

'Matti! Desmond! Hop to. No more soaking up the blankets. Hop to.'

Every morning it is the same. He rouses them from their sleep, dragging them from their beds by the peremptory authority of his voice. Sleepy, unwilling children. He flexes his fingers with impatience. 'Hop to. Hurry up. Come on.' (Early on, once, Matti had not come on. She had lingered, huddling in the warmth under the blankets and, lo and behold, her father had thrown a jug of cold water in her face. The sense of shock and helplessness had left her crawling with shame and every morning his voice reminds her and she quivers in humiliation again.)

The children hop to. Within three minutes they are seated silently in the car, clutching their towels. Matti tugs and wiggles herself in her bubble cossie, tying and untying the straps so that they will be just right, not too tight and not too loose around her neck, and somehow help her swim.

Down the hill they drive and turn towards the bay. Matti shivers. Every morning she shivers. And snuffles. And wishes she could disappear in the eerie stillness of the light that hangs, glistening and hypnotic, over the water. But there is no time for dreams of disappearing. The car has come to a halt beside the park and Dr Milton has snapped off the ignition. Quick-sticks. There is work to be done.

Matti sidles uneasily through the turnstiles, treading carefully on the rickety boards that form a walkway around the pool. Looking down through the boards at the water, slicked with a rainbow of oil, makes her feel queasy. She hopes for a miracle. A splinter, a croupy cough, a dog. But there is no miracle. Ever. Slowly, slowly, she draws off her jumper, reties her straps and starts to tuck her curls under her bathing cap.

'Hurry up, Matti. No dilly-dallying.'

'But Mummy said not to get my hair wet. I have to tuck it under.' The fingers flex again. Matti knows what that means.

'In you go now. Let's not have any more delay this morning.'

Matti starts to cry. She hides behind Desmond as he starts for the steps.

'None of that now. In you go. Dive in. Head first.'

'No, Daddy, please. No, I'll be good today. I'll do the breathing and everything. Please. Just let me go in down the steps. Please.'

'Matti! At once.'

Desmond has already dived. Sullenly, each morning, he will go through his paces.

'Please, Daddy. No! Please.' Matti's voice rises to a shout of fear as her father cracks his knuckles in annoyance, reaches over, and with one hand, up-ends her. Grasping each ankle, he holds her suspended over the cold, dark water. Her screams prevent her holding her breath so that when he lets her go she falls and swallows her first mouthful. Up she comes, spluttering, and paddles frantically for the steps. But he is there before her and fends off her grasping hands with his foot.

'Now, Matti. I won't stand any more of this. I want over-arm today. Proper breathing. Head well in. Off you go.'

'Please, Daddy. Let me get my breath for just a minute. Please. I got a mouthful.'

'You haven't even started yet. Off you go or we'll have to go down the other end.'

Her voice becomes shrill with terror.

'No. Please. I'll do it.' She paddles herself around and faces the distance. The far, far steps. She kicks and waves her arms and ducks her head in and out, gasping. Desmond passes her, stolidly doing his laps. After an eternity of streaming water and confusion, her lungs bursting, she lunges for the far steps. Once again he is there before her.

'I'm sorry, Matti, but this will not do. Back you go, breathing properly this time.'

'Please, Daddy. No. No.' They look at each other, he towering darkly above her, a colossus, wills battling. 'I can't.'

'You can and you will.' Her eyes stinging, treading water, she blinks up at him. He looms like some giant of the beanstalk, his eyes hard with fury.

'Very well, my dear. I'm sorry but you force me to be firm.' Quick as a flash he reaches down and hauls her by the back of her cossie from the water. Never lessening his grip, he drives her stumbling before him to the shallow end of the pool.

'Now, my dear. Down you go and let's make this as quick as possible.' Matti stands rooted to the spot and screams. His patience snaps. Briskly he pulls her down the steps. Seating himself behind her, he bends forward and grasps her calves. With a wrenching jerk he topples her and she falls forward into the water, still screaming.

'In. Out. In. Out.' Dr Milton chants the breathing rhythm as he holds her legs rigid and twists her body, first to the side then face down into the water. 'In. Out. In. Out.' Matti gasps and chokes, swallowing the salty water. I'm drowning, she thinks. He's drowning me. She fights against him but his grip is relentless. Every so often she gulps a breath, no longer knowing which way lie sky and air. Finally she goes limp in his hands. Exhausted. No fight left. Defeated.

That is what he has been waiting for.

'That is all for this morning, Matti. Run and get your towel, my dear. Let us hope we do not have to have a repetition of this unpleasantness. It hurts your old Dad, you know, to have to do this.' Matti pulls herself up the steps, her eyes bleary, her cap askew. As she comes she retches the salty burning water through her nose and mouth.

Her body is weak and exhausted and consumed with hatred. *I hate you. I hate you. I hate you with your quiet voice and your white sluggy legs, all hairy, and your rude pink titties. I hate you. I hate you. I wish I could kill you. I'd stab you into a million bits so that slimy things fell out of your tummy and I'd jump on them so they would squash and squelch and I'd be glad and I'd specially get your tongue out so that you couldn't talk in that sad quiet voice and tell me how I hurt and disappoint you and how hard it is for you and everything. And I'd pop out your eyes and . . .* She drags herself onto the walkway and watches him drying his back. *I wish you'd die so I don't have to do this ever again. Didn't have to swallow burning water and vomit it out of my nose and . . .*

Dr Milton rubs her back briskly with her towel and drags off her cap so it makes a sucking noise and her hair catches and pulls like a million needles. I hate you, she thinks. *I hate you and I wish you were dead. And do you hate me? Do you hate me so much that you would drown me?*

Her body shakes with cold and the wickedness of her thoughts. Desmond comes down to join them.

'All right, giblets,' calls Dr Milton, moving off at a jog. 'Twice around the oval, then home for brekka.'

The three of them run. When it is done they return panting to the car.

'Bags I sit in the front,' yells Matti. 'I bags sit next to Daddy.'

It is very important for Matti to separate her worlds. It is too confusing if she does not. She must not let the early morning swims intrude into life at home. Once they are over, everything must be absolutely normal. She must not talk to Mummy about what happens. How could Mummy help? How could Mummy even understand? After all, Mummy cannot swim! Daddy had pointed out that it is not her fault, being brought up in the bush, but certainly it is unfortunate and Mummy is to be pitied because of it. Nonetheless, inside Matti, deep in, certain feelings refuse to separate. She grows taut and anxious even if the word 'swim' is just

49

mentioned. Time and again, although she pushes and pushes, the feeling comes to her that she is afraid of Daddy. That she hates him. Surely not. She must try harder.

The Miltons eat a substantial breakfast. It is important to have a good start to the day. Mrs Milton has fried the bacon and eggs, grilled the sausages, put toast in toast racks, butter and butter knives in dishes, jam in little pots with tiny jam spoons that Matti loves.

They sit in the dining-room at the long table with the yellow tablecloth and matching serviettes. The baby is propped up in a high chair beside Matti, who spoons farex into his mouth as she prepares to eat her own breakfast. It is formal and orderly and business-like as well. People have appointments to keep.

Matti is loving the predictability of it all. The baths have been very unpleasant this morning. Here in the dining room is how everything should be. Dr Milton is not so pleased with things. He is angry. Very angry. The morning's unpleasantness wastes a great deal of time. Dr Milton does not have time to waste. There are patients awaiting him, work to be done. He will not be thwarted. Not by a wilful little girl. Not by anyone. It will not be tolerated.

Matti takes the plate that her mother passes to her, cuts the meat and takes a mouthful. The taste is so unexpected, so horrid, that without thinking, she spits it out.

'Eat your liver, Matti!' says her father quietly.

'I don't like it', she says. Oh, Matti. She is more surprised than anything else. She has never been a fussy eater.

'Eat your food at once. I will not tolerate any more unpleasantness this morning.' Matti stiffens. Her neck prickles. So he does remember this morning? So it does count with him, back here in the real world. 'Eat up at once. Your mother slaves in the kitchen for us all. Learn to be like her, Matti. Eat your breakfast. You are holding me up.'

Matti toys with the loathsome meat. She moves it round the plate, tastes the gravy, cuts little slivers off the corners, cuts and re-cuts. Suddenly . . .

'Matti. Open your mouth.' Her father holds her nose and forces a spoonful down her throat. Matti feels her throat lock. She is unable to swallow. The food rushes out again, down her uniform.

In disgust she moves to stand and clean herself. His hand presses hard upon her shoulder. He forces her to sit.

'Again please Matti.' The nose is pinched, the spoon jammed into her mouth. She coughs, chokes. Food lodges high up in her throat, behind her nose. Silent, hiccup-like retches come from her. He stuffs another spoonful in. It meets the mess she is attempting to spit out. In fury he drops the spoon onto the table and takes her face in his hands. In a passion of silent power, he holds her jaws closed, but not even his strength can withstand her physical loathing. The food explodes out of her nose and mouth as she wrenches her head from his clasp, spraying the table and her clothing.

The family sit silently, watching.

His voice now is weary.

'Mummy, Matti is to sit here until she eats her breakfast. Is that clear?' Matti sits. Daddy leaves. Desmond leaves. The meat is cold and hard and curling at the edges like old leather.

'Please Matti. Be a good girl. Eat up. You'll be late for school. Come on. Hurry up,' pleads Mummy.

'I can't. It makes me sick.' She starts to cry. Her mother sighs and mops the faces of the little boys and herds them out. She too is angry. Why can't Matti just do as she is told? Doesn't she know her father by now? There is no point in defying him. Matti is causing needless upset to them all. If there are 'words' tonight Mrs Milton thinks she will scream. He's impossible. It's her daughter's fault. Mrs Milton could run for miles.

Irritably the mother goes through the motions. Butter goes back into the butter box in the fridge. Little dishes of jam are scraped back into their jars. Cereal is returned to its packet, milk is carefully poured back into its bottle. The table is stripped of its cloth, the salt and pepper returned to the chiffonier and the fine old wood table wiped and dried and polished while Matti sits, locked to her chair. *Please help me, Mummy, please.*

After a time her mother speaks to her.

'Leave it, Matti. Run and get your bag. You'll catch the late tram if you hurry.' Matti pushes back her chair and rises. A violent force pushes her back down.

'I'm sorry, Mummy. But I must insist. I thought I made myself clear. I asked Matti to eat the breakfast that you had worked hard to prepare for us all and I return home to find she has not done so.' He turns to the girl. 'Perhaps now you see the selfish, deceitful, underhand measure of your ways. You attempt slyly to disobey, you hinder me from getting on with my work and you are holding up your mother.'

Matti sits with her head bowed. She cannot believe that eating the liver is more important to him than his patients so that he has actually left them and come home to see that he has been obeyed. Is she as wicked as that? It would seem so. But she cannot eat the food.

She sits until mid-morning before the loathsome meal. Finally, with immense sadness etched on his face, Dr Milton releases her from the chair.

'You may get your school bag, Margaret-Anne. Mother McPhee will want to know why you are late. I shall take you myself and tell...'

'Oh no! Please don't tell. Please.'

'Mother McPhee must be made aware of your defiant ways.'

Matti looks at him in horror. She hears a huge door slamming shut forever. The thudding of her heart tells her that something terrible has happened. Images flash before her eyes, flash and recede, flash and recede, growing ever fainter. Images of yellow and white and radiant light, images of great and joyful tumult. Over her mind another image settles, of dread, of great brooding silence, of cold and ice. It seems to Matti as she drives silently to school with him, that she is actually far far out on a huge ice-field, and even if she were to shout very loudly, no one would ever hear, or be able to understand her words. Even if they wanted to reach her they couldn't because the ice is breaking up all around her, leaving her quite marooned, alone on her ice floe. He is leaving her ever more alone. He is abandoning her in impossible places where she does not want to go. He is spreading the poison of her ways. Betraying her. Soon all who think her lovely and special and blessed will discover what a bad, ungrateful, selfish, defiant girl she is. A troublesome creature who saddens all who love her and are doing things for her own good.

Her mind careers frantically. Perhaps if I try to be really perfect, they will never believe him, they will never find out. But what about me? screams the hateful Matti. What about me who hates him? Who would like to kill him. No, no, I love him. I do. I'll show him. I'll try so hard that he will love me like before.

The car slides to a halt. She gets out, afraid to look at him, so ruthlessly does he ignore her. *Please Daddy, please love me. You do love me, don't you?*

SIX

Mother McPhee watches her charges with the alert eyes of a mother. She sighs sometimes when she thinks of Matti. The change was so sudden. After that morning when her father dropped her so inexplicably late. Growing up she supposes, when she has time to dwell on it. There is something withdrawn, intensely watchful, about the child now. Not that her behaviour is any less pleasing than before. If anything, more so. There's less of the disruptive high spirits. Her lessons are well learnt, her homework impeccable, her memorising outstanding, her manner courteous and her attitude exemplary. If Mother McPhee were to criticise, perhaps she would point to a need, a tension, to excel. But perhaps she would not. Her ethos, the ethos of the school, the ethos of the parents who entrust their daughters to the nuns, is towards excellence. A good thing. Matti is excelling herself.

Reverend Mother's feast is approaching. The entire school, seniors and juniors, combine in a Wishing for her. It always takes the form of tableaux to illustrate the saints, or history, or costumes, or great plays. There is a lot of singing and flowers and book displays and art displays and music. Very good, very special, very lucky girls are chosen for the tableaux. Matti is among the chosen.

Mother Porter, the Mistress of Drama in the Senior School, phones Mrs Milton.

'Mrs Milton, we are preparing Reverend Mother's Wishing and hope you will lend us Margaret-Anne for two or three nights.' Lend her! Like some precious possession. Mummy packs a small bag with night clothes and, for the duration, when lessons finish each afternoon, Mother McPhee leads Matti through Nazareth, along the passage by the piano cells, up the stairs from Marble Square and deposits her in the senior study room where some seniors have been deputised to care for her.

They fuss about her. The change from their rigid routine delights them. Matti is their baby. Matti! The big one at home. She submits to their ministrations as they brush her hair and hold her hand and take her to the infirmary for chocolate milk and buns. And after supper they take her to the hall where the Wishing is being prepared. Mother Porter fits her with a variety of costumes and places her on the stage where she stands motionless while lights are adjusted and effects are discussed. It is easy for her to submit, easy to remain motionless, easy to be silent, for she can almost believe that the spotlights shining down are shining just for her. That she is at the very centre of all that is important. She belongs, she is needed, and the glow and heat and depth of the lights warm her, almost melting icy uncertainties that she holds buried, deep down. There is nothing to fear here. In her school life. The rules never change. She knows them by heart. It is easy to be certain. She does not have to be forever on the alert.

The juniors make their way down to the pool at the end of the day's lessons, towels and cossies and caps in plastic beach bags. They line up outside Nazareth and, leaning over the wall, can see, far below, tucked modestly in the bush, the square of water, surrounded by the high paling fence. Mother McPhee signals and they plunge down the first flight of stone steps, through the grotto, down, down, down, single file now on the rough track into the bush, part scrub, part rainforest. Here they go past the nuns' laundry, giggling and nudging each other at the sight of row upon row of black lisle stockings and swami underpants, flapping huge and shapeless in the breeze.

On they go, slithering in the muddy part under the evil-smelling chook yard where the guano is thick upon the ground, elbowing aside the heavy stand of cannas that conceal the entrance to the pool and come to an untidy and excited halt at the gates. Mother McPhee says the recreation prayer and they surge through and disappear into the cubicles that surround the pool. They tear off their clothes and drag on cossies in the race to be first in. Doors explode open and the human bullets fire themselves through the air and into the water. Splashes and shrieks punctuate the air as they hurtle about or drag themselves in exhaustion from the water to flop, streaming, onto the concrete surrounds. But not for long. They know that Mother McPhee will tinkle the bell and gesture, for rules say, no lolling about, no sunbaking or displaying the body immodestly or vainly, at the pool. (Oh, the outrage and the hurried note home the day that little Marilyn Moss jumped in, in the leopard-skin cossie that had no top!)

Oh, yes, school is delicious and predictable, but one morning, as Matti swings through the door she sees Mother McPhee standing, severely, before the children. They are very silent.

'Now that you are all assembled, I would ask the child responsible for this, to come forward.' She turns to the blackboard and swings it over. There before them is an ugly drawing of Patricia Mary, the fattest girl in the Junior School. The girls sneak glances at each other and giggle behind their hands. Clack, clack, clack goes the carved wooden signal in Mother McPhee's hand. They fall silent.

'I have never before witnessed such a disgusting exhibition. There will be no Christian Doctrine this morning. I shall be in my study. The child or children responsible will bring themselves to me and own up.' She turns, wipes the offending picture in a flurry of chalk dust from the board and walks away, the heavy wooden rosary beads at her side clinking and clanking.

Poor Mother McPhee. She waits in vain. The long morning drones on and no one comes to see her. At lunch time the girls are permitted to sit down but they must remain absolutely silent and she stands on surveillance over them. If there was ever a moment for the culprit to step forward it has long since passed. Afternoon lessons are cancelled and they sit silently with Christian Doctrine books before them.

Next morning Matti hurries with her usual happy anticipation to school. Mother McPhee makes the rounds of all the classrooms.

'Reverend Mother has been informed of this unpleasantness.' Matti's scalp prickles. Unpleasantness. Is that not what Daddy is constantly distressed by? 'She has decided, in her wisdom, that the pool will be closed to the entire Junior School until the child or children responsible owns up. Whoever is responsible is now punishing the whole school.'

Gossip and rumour are rife and corrosive. The longer the uncertainty lasts, the more uneasy Matti becomes. Her mind whirls with anxiety and she seeks to delve for some transgression she has committed. Could it be possible that she is the culprit and doesn't know it? Has she been mistaken in thinking that she is safe here? Are there traps everywhere, not just at home? She seeks among the faces around her to find, by look or word or deed, the actual culprit so she may be freed from the guilt and anxiety she feels. But she never finds her.

The pool is denied them all summer term.

'Please, Mother. Oh, please Mother. Can't we go? Please. It's not fair,' some of the braver ones plead. But Mother McPhee's face hardens and she says: 'The child responsible knows what she has to do.' They are puzzled, angry, rebellious. They know the time, the opportunity has passed. No one will ever own up now. They know this. Why not, Mother McPhee?

SEVEN

Flynn O'Brien is preparing to leave for Sacre Coeur in this, her final year of Junior School. Flynn doesn't know exactly why she is leaving the old convent but she does know that her exhausted mother believes that the European order might do something, with its refinement and culture, for her wild, undisciplined daughter. More anyway than the old Irish nuns with their cane and ruler. Who knows? Who cares? Flynn doesn't.

She is eleven years old and wearing a dreadful straw hat with cherries on it. Her mother, who seems always to be stirring a saucepan, with a baby on her hip and a telephone cradled under her ear, taking messages for her husband who has the surgery in the front of the house, simply hasn't had time to get Flynn's new uniform.

'Put on the pique, Flynn, and your gloves. Leave your hat on. It's lovely. Never mind, dear, we'll order your uniform from the convent.' Flynn is not the sort of child to make a fuss over something as silly as a dress. She shrugs and puts on the pique and follows her mother to the Sacre Coeur. She has no idea what to expect and is absolutely cheerful.

As usual, Mrs O'Brien is running late. Can't be helped. Bubbie was sick all over the pique when Flynn hugged her goodbye and the material needed a good sponging. Vomit is such a persistent smell. Mother Portress admits them through the Lodge and firmly dismisses Mrs O'Brien.

'Come along, my dear. Goodbye Mrs O'Brien. Goodbye.' And closes the huge door. Taking Flynn's hand she leads her down the dark corridors.

'You are late my dear. The school has already assembled for the reading of the School Rule as we do on the first day of each year. Reverend Mother has already arrived, so slip in quietly, curtsey to Reverend Mother and take a seat on the side.'

Curtsey! Flynn slips in, bobs and sits. She sees the timber-panelled hall, the shiny floorboards, the flowers arranged on the ground in front of Reverend Mother, and row upon row of strange faces, all motionless. She feels no shame in the dreadful hat. She looks about her with interest. The School Rule sounds like a lot of twaddle so she doesn't pay it much attention. Like a friendly, intelligent dog, uncomprehending but alert, she sniffs the air.

After a long time, the whole school rises with a collective sigh, a movement of air, and curtseys in perfect unison. Then a small nun makes a strange clacking sound and row by row they file silently out. Flynn feels a hand upon her arm.

'Join the ranks at the end, Flynn dear. The juniors go out last. In silence.' So she does and in silence because she doesn't yet know who to speak to or what about. She follows where she is led, enters a classroom and takes a seat.

'Settle down now children. It is so nice to have you all back with us, and our newcomer.' A nun smiles at them. 'We will start our new year with some reading around the class.' The girls open their readers. The nun comes towards Flynn.

'I'm Mother Leary, Flynn. Welcome to St Stanislaus. This is our room for the year and the Saint will be our special helper. All the rooms — page eighteen, children — are named after precious saints. Soon you will be familiar with our ways.' Flynn looks sceptical. She is a great one for devils and fairies and kidnappers but saints bore her a bit. So good. So holy. The nun looks pretty holy too, and very young. Younger than the old bats at the other convent. She wears the black habit and the pie-crust frill frames her face but instead of the black veil she wears what looks for all the world like a white sheet over her head. Soon Flynn will realise that she is a mere novice, still twelve months off getting her black veil.

Clack, clack, clack, goes the little signal.

'We'll begin. Around the class.' Flynn sits back comfortably. She is an excellent reader. This is a breeze. She tilts back on her chair and listens to the others as, paragraph about, they read the story.

Now the girl in front of her is reading. It is the adventures and challenges and trials of Loki and Thor and the Norsemen. This surprises Flynn. At the other school they only read holy stories. Then it is her turn and she reads easily, no mistakes. Then Mother Leary gives out the marks. Marks are given for everything in this school, as Flynn will soon discover. Matti comes top. She usually does. And, unexpectedly she peeps over her shoulder and looks at Flynn. She is very impressed that someone dressed like that and with the dreadful hat would have the confidence to attend the School Rule.

'Hello,' she whispers. 'What's that?'

'It's a pencil sharpener,' says Flynn. So it is. In the shape of an aeroplane with a rubber for a nose cone. 'You can have it if you like. Go on.' Mother Leary clacks sharply. Matti turns back to the front, head down to her book.

'Can I really?'

'Course.' Flynn lobs it neatly over her head and into Matti's lap.

Matti and Flynn discover that before and after school they share the tram journey while the others do not. They are collected by nannies and mummies in shiny cars but Matti and Flynn do not feel sorry for themselves. Oh, no indeed not. What a time they have of it on the rattly old tram even though they are so different really. Matti so good and neat and punctual and her parents so strict, and Flynn so slapdash and undisciplined. Every morning Flynn brings comics for Matti to read on the tram. There is no question of overnight loans. Has not Dr Milton forbidden them, along with the afternoon newspaper, as trash? But what wonderful trash! Stories of ice-skating stars, pony clubs, English boarding schools and bullies and midnight feasts and mad teachers. Intrepid girls intercept secrets, expose spies, run cafes, raise money for operations for dying mothers. Matti gobbles up the stories and they hide the comics behind the lantana before entering the school doors. No child may carry unauthorised reading matter into the school, say the rules.

Matti has done her bit too and converted Flynn to the saints, the most interesting bunch, that is. The virgin martyrs. Matti and

Flynn make up the most appalling tortures for them, the holy books being fairly vague.

'Do you think, if you were a virgin martyr, you would give in, Flynn?' asks Matti as they cross Nazareth on their way to collect their bags.

'Depends what they were going to do with me. I'd pretend to and try to escape when they weren't looking.'

'But I don't think the saints wanted to escape, did they? They wouldn't be saints if they ran away.'

'S'pose not.'

But escaping from communists is another thing altogether. You can escape from them and be a real hero. Flynn and Matti know a lot about communists. The nuns are constantly exhorting them to pray for all the poor people who live under communist rule. Matti and Flynn can quite easily imagine that one day they might be in danger of being under communist rule. After all, as the nuns say, without a great deal of prayer, it is only a matter of time. They prepare themselves.

Beside the old oil heaters outside Bethlehem they stand holding each other's hands for courage. They are to face interrogation. They are to be tortured until they recant and spit on the crucifix. 'You go first, Matti. I'll count.' Matti holds her fingers out until they touch the red hot pipes. 'One, two, three, four, fi ... You took your hand off. My turn.' Matti sucks her fingers and counts for Flynn. They get braver and braver until one day Matti blisters her fingers badly.

'No, I don't think I could be tortured until I died. But what I'd do, I'd pretend to recant and spit and everything, but I wouldn't really. God would know I was just pretending. Then they'd let me go but I'd still be a secret Catholic.'

'Mm ...' says Flynn.

They talk loudly on the tram in a gobbledygook tongue, waving their arms about, hoping that people will think they are foreign. Matti is excited with her new friend. Naturally, she cannot invite her home, but it's 'Flynn this', and 'Flynn that'. She can't help herself. Mummy and Daddy are not so sure that this new girl is going to be a good influence, and what a peculiar time for her to turn up at Sacre Coeur. Flynn sounds forceful. Mummy and Daddy fear undue influence. Flynn doesn't think of influencing anybody. She can't be bothered. Flynn is lazy, the nuns say. She thinks Matti is very clever and doesn't mind that Matti's work is singled out and held up as an example. If she wanted to she could have hers singled out too.

Matti never speaks about home to Flynn even when Flynn chatters away about Bubbie and pocket money and the Saturday arvo pictures up at the Randwick Ritz and how Mummy sings all the time in the kitchen—when the phone isn't ringing! Matti keeps home private. From everybody. When she can. She is ashamed about home. Today her report card has arrived. It is a model of application and good results and Mother Leary has added a tiny addendum. 'Matti must learn to take criticism with a better grace.' Dr Milton is most displeased.

'Well, my dear. There it is. You... Don't give me that look, my dear... You know that the sin of the angels was pride and you know what happened to Lucifer and his cohorts.' Matti stares at him. What is this nonsense he is talking, this comparison he is making? Why is he talking of the devil and fallen angels and hell? 'No, my dear, you know perfectly well what I am talking about.' A moment of raging fury, of rebellion, rises in her.

'I don't.'

'I think you do, Matti. This is, here and now, an example of your inability to take criticism. Precisely what the good Mothers are so disappointed about.' So disappointed? They're not so disappointed about anything.

'I don't understand,' she says sullenly.

'You know exactly what I am talking about,' says Dr Milton.

Matti stands before him. He speaks quietly, dispassionately, definitively. He is her parent. She has to believe him and, besides, isn't everyone always saying how wonderful he is? He's even been in the newspapers! Then she must be wrong. But she's not. How can she be? Surely, to be as wicked as Lucifer, to be thrown out of the Garden of Paradise, she would have to feel bad. I hate you, Daddy, whispers the voice. I hate you, hate you, hate you. Matti hangs her head in shame.

Dr Milton has thought long and hard about his daughter. She troubles him deeply. There is something furtive about her, something potentially rebellious. He will not be rebelled against. Why is she not open and forthcoming like her brothers? He remembers wistfully a golden, dancing child he met on a wharf long ago, a child with kisses and hugs and welcomes in abundance, with laughter and gladness in her face.

He sighs. Matti is his hair-shirt. She tires him. Pride and defiance must be stripped from her. Not for his good, but for hers. It is his duty as a father. If he cannot inculcate in her the basic and fundamental rules of selflessness and dedication that are required of a woman, then he will have failed as a father. Dr Milton does not countenance failure. And he will not be thwarted. He is used to getting what he wants, at any cost.

He tries again,

'Believe me, my dear, I find these little chats as unpleasant as you do. It hurts me far more than it hurts you but without the disciplines you will be an unhappy woman. Emulate your mother, Matti. Emulate your mother. For your old Dad. Do it for him. Remember, I'm on your side, Matti.'

He looks at the set face, the rigid jaw, the brimming eyes. Matti is unsure of what she wants to be, but of one thing she is sure: she does not want to be, will not be, like her mother. Her mother is burdened and powerless and Matti will not be that. He cannot change her mind. Dr Milton hardens his heart. Matti stares at him, unable to speak, the rebellion almost chokes her. Why does he talk to her all soft and gentle when his words have told her of outer darkness and hell? What does he want of her that she is not giving?

Just tell me once, that I do it well. Please. I need you to tell me you love me still.

The offending report is locked with solemn ceremony in his desk drawer, a wretched, disgraceful piece of paper to build up the dossier.

EIGHT

Matti attends to one of her little jobs. Her Sunday night job. She carries into Daddy his weekly bottle of beer on a silver tray and the disgusting stinking gorgonzola. The ritual never fails to please him. Oh, everything is hunky-dory, tickety-boo when she does things nicely. That is what he says.

Very well then. She thinks hard. She will not just sit back and hope she is pleasing him. She will find wonderful new ways to please him. Besides, something else is troubling her. She is afraid that he might forget her in this burgeoning household, full of active, noisy little boys who totally preoccupy Mummy and interest Daddy so much. What would be worse? To be left alone or to be forgotten? Matti could not bear to be forgotten. And she has a splendid way of making sure she is not.

The Miltons eat the evening meal together. It is a discipline that Dr Milton insists upon even though it frequently exhausts his wife, who would prefer to have some of the children in bed before the appointed dinner hour. Matti becomes the dinner-time entertainer. It seems to be working well, although her mother is not enthusiastic.

'Stop waving your arms about, Matti. You'd think you were an Italian, or something. Get on with your dinner.' But Matti knows her act amuses her father. His eyes twinkle and she plays for him and him alone. And now it is his turn. He reaches for the fruit knife and carves an orange peel into a huge set of teeth and turns away a moment then faces the table with huge teeth jutting from his mouth and one eye turned almost inside out. Little Brother squeals and knocks over his milk and Mrs Milton says, 'Please, Patrick,' and the doctor rolls back his eye and removes the teeth and winks at Matti and says gently to his wife. 'A little tomfoolery never hurt anyone, my dear.'

Mrs Milton looks angrily at Matti but Matti takes no notice.

Meal times too are a splendid opportunity to show off her memorising and Desmond, not to be outdone, challenges her, night after night, to long recitations from the books that they are reading—under their father's aegis.

Squire Trelawney, Doctor Livesey and the rest of these gentlemen have asked me to write down the particulars of Treasure Island from beginning to end, leaving nothing back but the bearings of the island and that because there is treasure not yet found. So I take up my pen in the year of grace 17— and go back to the time when my father owned the Admiral Benbow Inn and the old sea-dog with the sabre cut first took up his lodgings under my roof. I remember it as though it were yesterday...

'Matti. Desmond. Stop that please. Eat up quickly.' Their mother looks to the end of the table for support. She often complains that their father is 'miles away' and indeed he is. Carefully, vaguely, he slits the banana skin with his fruit knife, lays aside the fruit and cuts the skin into segments and eats it.

'Patrick!' Their mother's voice snaps through the air. He looks mildly around at their staring faces. He laughs. He picks up the skin and drapes what is left across his top lip and wiggles it. They giggle in delight. It is delicious. Matti never wants it to end. This is her real Daddy, the one she loves so much, the person it is often so hard to find. This is really Daddy. Let this go on for ever and ever and ever.

'Our singing teacher, Miss Mort, has psittacosis,' she says. Her little brothers listen carefully. 'Yes, she has these huge legs like tree trunks and...'

'No, Matti. Not psittacosis,' says her father vaguely.

'But Daddy, they are all wrinkly and hanging down and...'

'Elephantiasis,' he mutters vaguely, his mind elsewhere again.

('My father says Miss Mort has elephantiasis' Matti tells the class and it becomes fact.)

Matti is getting more and more cunning. He has entreated her to walk like a little lady. He tells her she walks like a sailor. Often, when she passes, he whistles a hornpipe. So deeply does this humiliate her she makes a little blue and white sailor cap for herself and incorporates a sailor routine into her table behaviour. The doctor is pleased to see that Matti is learning to be a good sport.

Nevertheless sometimes he is unfair, just too unfair. She knows already that he is concerned by her table manners. He has a signal for her.

'It's only men in rags and gluttons steeped in sin, Who treat themselves like carpetbags and shovel victuals in.'

She hears, she slows down her eating. It's a private, all-good-sports joke. So how can he use it against her like this? It is Saturday night. The night of the crumbed cutlets, with white frilled collars, standing around a castle of mashed potato encircled by a moat of peas. Matti's mouth waters. It is her favourite meal. She helps her mother serve out for the family and the two priests who have come as usual for Saturday dinner. From place to place she goes, delivering food, offering sauce, cutting up meat for the little fellows.

Finally she and her mother are served. In glorious anticipation she packs her fork. Meat, potato, now the peas, studded to stick to the potato and over all, a smear of sauce. She raise fork to mouth, she bends, concentrating.

'It's only men in rags, Matti.'

She swallows, she ducks her head and blushes. The food sticks to her palate. She glances quickly at the priests. Have they heard?

'And gluttons steeped in sin.' His voice is lyrical now, almost dreamy. He is smiling, enjoying himself. She wriggles uncomfortably, wills him to silence, hates him.

'Who treat themselves like... Oh, Father, you've finished.

Offer Father more meat please, my dear,' he says to his wife, who has only just started her meal.

Matti continues to eat carefully, all pleasure fled.

Da da dum pom pom
Da da dadadada dum
He whistles. She jigs along, smiling jaunty sailor. She knocks over the coffee table as she hornpipes past.

'Oh, my dear. Life's not all beer and skittles. You can't clown all your life, Matti. Try and be a bit more ladylike. Poor old Matti. Front-row forward legs. Poor old Matti.'

She flinches away from him, loathing herself and her great, lumbering inadequacies.

'Shoulders back. Remember Quasimodo.'

She turns, stumbles from the room, sailor cap a crumpled bundle in her hand.

She does not hear her mother and father talking.

'Leave her alone, Patrick. She's not fat. She's not clumsy. She's got your legs, that's all. She can't help that. And...'

'My dear girl...'

'No, Patrick. And do you realise that she won't sing in the choir? That's your fault too, Patrick. You told her her voice was terrible...'

'My dear girl, don't talk arrant nonsense. Matti's sulkiness has nothing to do with me. Matti must learn to take criticism like a good sport. It is for her own good. She and I have our little jokes. She enjoys them.'

Mrs Milton returns to her mending. Take criticism like a good sport. Could *he*? He's a bully, that's what he is. Defending her daughter has exhausted her. As if she hasn't got enough to do. She is angry at her daughter. The sooner Matti learns that a woman's lot in life is one of sacrifice, oh, not gladly but bitterly given, the better off she will be. She must realise that she can change nothing. This is how it always was and always will be. You can't argue with men.

She has more to concern her anyway. The little lump. It is to be removed. Matti has known that there have been subdued phone conversations. Friends of Daddy have come over and talked to him quietly. Mummy looks tired. Daddy looks worried.

'Matti, tomorrow Mummy is going into hospital for a little op and you are going to be in charge. I want you to be a great help.'

'Yes, I will, Daddy. What's wrong. Is she . . .?' Going to die?

'Nothing to worry about. Just a little op. Be a good girl.'

Granny arrives, hunched and bunned and worried. She must be going to die.

'Oh Matti darling, don't worry, Granny's here. I'll look after you.' But Daddy sends Matti off to bed, quick smart.

The next day is strange and empty. No parents in the house. Granny down at the church. Just a little op? Nothing to worry about? Why all this then? But here comes Daddy, swinging up the path, smiles, whistles. Matti's heart sings. He's back. It's going to be all right. He will explain everything. And Granny comes through the gate.

'Thanks be to God and St Anthony, Patrick! Hallelujah!' Granny advances on Matti, sweeps her into her arms, against her soft bosom.

'Oh, darling, it's all right. Mummy is going to be well. Thank God. You must have been so worried.'

'It's all right, Granny,' snaps her father. 'Matti knew nothing about it.'

Matti puts her brothers to bed. She reads to them. She cuddles and kisses them and turns off the light. Her jobs are done. She takes herself to bed and climbs under the covers. She tries hard not to think about Mummy. She realises all the little things that make Mummy's presence real, like the sound of her sandals clipping on the brown lino outside the kitchen, and the little sniffs that she has to give when she hasn't got a hand free to reach for a hanky for her eternally dripping nose, or the sight of her in the flower pantry, burning the stalks of the poppies or cutting the hydrangeas, and the sound of her bath running late at night. How incomplete the house feels without her. They are the things that mean 'Mummy' to Matti. Why didn't Daddy share about Mummy? You're a horrible mean man. You are. You are. Matti is lonely.

Her hand slips to the comfort between her legs. She strokes herself gently. So warm. So warm. She wiggles her fingers inside her flaps of skin. She pats gently. So warm.

As Daddy says, and everyone knows, Matti can do anything she sets her mind to. Just about. She wants to be a ballerina and be able to stand on her tiptoes in pale pink toe-shoes and wear a tutu like a cloud of glittering raindrops. But one thing that Matti is certainly not good at is ballet. She knows it but she doesn't tell anyone. Once a week she goes to the studio and changes into her black bubble pants and white singlet and lumbers around on her big fat footballer legs and is mortified by her grossness next to all the little fairies.

Then she is a naughty girl. She wants to be sure to catch Flynn's tram and won't help Mummy fold the sheets in the linen pantry.

'Be a good girl, Matti. Help me.'

'But Mummy, I'll be late. Ask Desmond. You never ask him to do anything.'

'Come on Matti.'

'I'll be late. I can't.' She backs out of the cramped space and a hand like the bite of a bulldog grips her shoulder.

'Apologise to your mother at once, and get to. I did not believe that the day would come when I would hear you speak like that to your mother. That's the end of the ballet for you, my dear.'

With what a bad grace she helps her mother. Tired mother. Overworked mother. Suffering mother! *Well, I never asked you to suffer. I never asked you to slave, as you call it. Why do you? Just stop, why don't you? I won't slave. Not ever. I'll never slave for anyone.*

Fold and fold again, step forward, step back, step forward again, and a perfectly folded sheet. And now the next one. While he prowls out there. *Hate you. Hate you. Snooping and listening and watching and waiting, like God doling out the penances. Hate you. And her! Why doesn't she fight? I will. I will.*

Matti attends ballet class that afternoon. The best part about going is the old building whose one lift has to be helped up with a rope. It's noisy and dark and pianos tinkle on every floor. (One day Margot Fonteyn had been rehearsing there and the students had taken turns peeping through the key hole until they had been shooed away.) She moves around the studio waving ungainly arms, lumpish, dreaming she is a ballerina, mortified by her clumsiness. Miss Laurel is pounding her cane on the floor to the thump thump of the piano. Miss Laurel hates them all, fat little elephants. She flicks the cane against thighs and calves and ankles and turned-over insteps.

The door opens and the piano hesitates and dies and there is Daddy, grim and meaning business, beckoning Miss Laurel and the two of them are talking. Matti is aghast. She pretends she doesn't know him. She twirls her foot and stares towards the ceiling. She shrugs her ignorance.

'Margaret-Anne. Go with your father please.' She baulks a moment, tucks her singlet into the loathsome bubble pants then steps towards him.

Another silent journey. No sign, no glimmer. Whirling, ghost-like figures, clouds of tulle, puffs of white, blow light and inconsequential as smoke across her mind. She hates the man with a passion of murderous hate but this time she experiences the sweet whiff of victory too. Ha. Ha. Ha. I've got a secret, I won't tell and I don't care if you go to hell.

Dr Milton drives his daughter home seething with resentment and fury at her disruptive, disobedient ways. How dare she attend ballet class after he has expressly told her there is to be an end to it? He will not accept her rudeness and her laziness. If necessary he will have to cut out her every treat. Matti huddles in the car hating him and laughing at the miracle that has freed her from the humiliating failure of ballet class.

NINE

Matti prefers to read books like the *Famous Five* and ballet books and horse books, books in which she can imagine it's her having the adventures, her being famous, her being the best at everything. Desmond prefers the classics and although Matti has done the reading Daddy requires, she can never imagine herself in books like *The Dog Crusoe* or *White Fang* or *Pickwick Papers*. She and Desmond have less in common these days but they no longer quarrel and Matti admires her brother tremendously. Desmond is exceptionally clever. In fact he has skipped a class, he is so clever. Matti hates being bored and finds she is bored a lot at home. You're never bored if you're busy, says Mummy. Desmond goes looking for hard work, says Daddy, and Matti knows that what they mean is that she is lazy. Matti feels inadequate compared to Desmond, but she still likes him.

Once in a while they share things and it is wonderful. Off they go, to the theatre.

'Are they really famous, Desmond?'

'Yes, they are the most famous actors in the world. They've been in lots of films too. Mummy says she went to a Sacre Coeur school in England and they're married but not in a Catholic church because they were divorced before.'

'Why did they get married twice?'

'Don't be silly, Matti. They were married to other people and got divorced.'

'Oh.'

Divorced. And from Sacre Coeur too! Matti is dying to see these famous people and scurries along beside her brother, clutching the bag of lollies they're allowed to eat in the theatre. They cross the railway bridge and descend the steps to the grimy old theatre. Desmond stations Matti at the staircase while he buys a programme. Matti's heart thumps inside her flat chest as she gazes at the photographs and the twinkling chandeliers and the heavy red curtains and the niches on the walls with little plaster heads sitting in them.

'Come on, Matti. When we sit down I'll explain it to you.' Matti is warm with happiness. Gravely Desmond outlines the play and Matti listens, wriggling in excitement and impatience.

And this is it! The lights dim and the theatre becomes a blanket of breath-holding darkness and suddenly the curtains sweep up and Matti goes to Venice. Her chest is tight with wonder. She cannot absorb the colours, the lights, the rhythmic voices, the dresses, the ruffles and the famous, beautiful people. Matti watches. She believes in it. She wants to be part of it. She is part of it.

Intervals interrupt. Time and again. Desmond reads from the programme. Matti no longer needs to hear. She is afraid of Shylock, in awe of Portia, suffering with Jessica, terrified for the cunning of it, transported.

'A pound of flesh. From the place nearest the heart...' She can hardly believe such dreadfulness. 'And therefore lay bare thy bosom.' A flush of heat races through her body, centres between her legs. She shivers, ticklish. 'Lay bare thy bosom.' The rudeness of it! She glances quickly at Desmond. He is still and attentive. Is he feeling it too? She tenses her body, feeling the excited pulsing, and stares at the stage. The man removes his shirt and Shylock approaches with the knife. Matti clamps her legs together in an agony of excitement and terror. Imagine! 'Lay bare thy bosom.'

It is over. The applause thunders around her head and she dreams it is she who is standing on the stage in her dress of pink silk and pearls, her head tall and proud and beautiful above the white ruffles at her neck. She is a throbbing hot body, every nerve end singing. She has fallen in love. Desmond has to drag her from the theatre, she dawdles so.

Matti is dreamy at home. Mummy is not sure she did the right thing, persuading Daddy to let them go to the Shakespeare. At any rate, Desmond is sent off alone to *Richard III*, just in case.

Matti tends to over-react to things and not get on with her jobs, says Mummy.

At every chance Matti sneaks off to Daddy's gloomy study and takes the Shakespeare from the shelf and leafs through the pages until she finds the lines, and all the wonders of the magical afternoon come back to her. 'Lay bare thy bosom.' She grows hot, and cocks her ear in case she is discovered.

The visit to the theatre has indeed affected Matti. Sometimes, she cannot say why, she needs to be by herself, away from the little boys, away from everyone. All alone. It's the strangest feeling that comes over her, as if she is drifting to a very quiet, still place. And when this happens she creeps to the kitchen and takes an egg cup and fills it with icing sugar. She dips her tongue into it, being careful not to breathe on it or it will puff up in a sneeze cloud under her nose. Carefully she carries her egg cup up the back stairs and opens the old suitcase that lies on the top landing. In it are all sorts of clothes. Some are Mummy's from a long time ago and some belong to aunts from the olden days. Carefully she sifts through until she finds one she wants. A chiffon dress with sparkling beads and a jagged hemline. She slips it over her head. It smells of dust and sometimes the weight of it causes it to tear. It is fragile as a cobweb. Holding it up with one hand, Matti picks up her icing sugar and creeps back to the stairs. Down she goes, to the spot, almost half way, where the gloom is deepest and there she sits. What she thinks she cannot say. It is enough to finger the chiffon gently between her thumb and forefinger and lick by lick taste the morsels of icing sugar, powdery and sweet on her tongue.

No one knows that Matti does this because she has picked her secret spot carefully and can hear if anyone is coming and run quickly upstairs and be standing beside the dressing-up case, just playing dress-ups. And when her secret game is over she rises with her empty egg cup and trails back up the stairs to remove the dress. Often she feels sleepy, as if she has come from a long way after a hard journey.

But she is not careful enough. Dr Milton, quiet as quiet in soft, suede shoes, discovers her. He comes upon her one Saturday afternoon when the rest of the house is still.

'Ah, Matti!' She shrinks from the dangerous heartiness in his voice. A fluttering butterfly pinned to the stairs. 'I have been looking for you, my dear. I am troubled by the amount of time you spend indoors. Fresh air and exercise, Matti. I've spoken often of it, as you and your brothers well know. Mens sana in corpore sano, Matti. Fresh air and exercise. All work and no play makes Jack . . . Ah, Matti, need I say more?' *Go away, leave me alone with my magic and my mystery and peace, snooping, bully man.*

'Oh, and one more thing, Matti. From now on my dear, I would like you to write me a precis of every book you read. Pleasure without discipline is laziness, and I want you to lick your laziness now. If you do not, you will find yourself a lonely and unhappy woman. Remember what I've said. Just leave the precis on my desk in the study and we can have a little chat about each book.'

He smiles at his daughter and climbs past her up the stairs. Matti sits very still. Her heart thuds and it frightens her. *What am I scared of?* Around her she sees the ice splintering. She sits still as still in order not to overbalance. The world outside the windows, the calls from her brothers, belong to a faraway place. In her world she is the only person, the only person in a glaring silver-black landscape, silent except for the creaking of ice. The chasms gape at her. She must not move.

Dusk falls as she sits alone. As from an endless, exhausting journey she comes home. She knows that she had lost the right to something that long, long ago gave her great comfort. For ever after the comfort will be tainted. She gets to her feet, lifts the dress over her shoulders, black dots enlarging and fading before her eyes. She shakes her head, reasserts herself, and creeps through the darkening house to her chores in the kitchen.

Her mother and father stand at the old scrubbed table as she enters.

'I've been calling you for ages,' says her mother. 'I had to run the bath myself. Go upstairs and get the little boys bathed. Quickly.'

'Just a minute,' says her father coldly. 'How dare you sulk after my words? Let me make one thing clear. I will not tolerate your selfishness. Root it out. Root it out. Let this be the last time I am forced to refer to it.' He dismisses her with a turning away of his face.

Mummy, Mummy, can't you hear him? Can't you help? I've done nothing to you. Have I? But her mother has her back to her, angrily scrubbing the potatoes. She creeps up the stairs, torn and terrified by the loneliness, unable to comprehend how the steamy humid bathroom and the pink, soapy bodies of her laughing brothers can belong to the same world that she is forced to inhabit.

Never again will she sit in her private place, and finger the cloth and taste the sweetness. Never again will she read a book openly in the house. She will read secretly and guiltily, sometimes hidden behind the pantry door, listening all the time for footsteps that will interrupt her at her unhealthy practice. In dry and barren words she writes a precis from time to time and leaves it on his desk, for his comments, but despite her waiting and her anxiety, he keeps her waiting forever.

TEN

Dr Milton is a driven man. He has decided on his course in life. Nothing will be allowed to interfere with that. His wife understands this, his colleagues understand this, his underlings understand this. Life and death, that is what his life is about. He can brook no selfishness, no shirking, no hindrance. Those who are caught up in the dazzle of his determination and drive stay around to cherish the kudos and excitement that come increasingly often now. Those who are not as enthralled, preferring freedom to total domination, leave him. This is how he would want it. He will not tolerate half-heartedness. Only the single-minded are among the elect. They stay gladly. The others escape.

Except the wife. The dutiful wife. Who must accept submission and martyrdom. Who screams soundlessly in anger and pain. And now, almost unbelievably, there is to be another child. She cannot accept this. She cannot survive another child. She believes she will go out of her mind at the thought of the swollen veins, the nausea, the heavy drag of the belly, the tearing, disgusting humiliation of birth with the attendant blood and pain and obscene interventions. She knows that her insides will come streaming out in exhaustion and tornworn death if this goes on. But it must go on. For her there is no choice. The child will come to term and be presented to her for her nurture and care and another life sentence will be added to her burdens. Who will help her? There is no one. It is her job, her ordained role, it is how it has always been and always must be. Her daughter will know of this duty one day and the wife cannot bear to look at the promise that will shrink and submit and dry out and die. She is filled with a mindless, inexplicable fury when she sees her daughter defying, refusing to submit. There is no escape. Better to know it now. Meanwhile she tells no one about the growing thing inside her aching belly.

Summer holidays. Cicada-ridden days. Fun and laughter and ignorance. They have played Cocky-Laura all afternoon, Matti and her brothers and her father. How happy Matti is. He has chosen her for his team and how she has raced and dodged and skidded and dived and helped her team to victory. 'Well done, partner,' he has said, shaking her hand. 'Now hop on in and help Mummy with the afternoon tea.'

And in she has hopped, pleased, so pleased that he has not only witnessed, but shared with her the victory. She races to the kitchen, a winner. She hurries to lay out the glasses and cups. Her mother watches her. She wrinkles her nose. In distaste. 'You smell, Matti' she says harshly. In an instant the triumph fails away and the girl stands speechless before her mother, her body crawling in disgust at her sudden filth. She longs for her mother to speak further. To tell her what to do about it. She can now, herself, smell the rancid, oniony smell from her armpits and she is revolted and recoils from herself. 'Go and wash,' is all the mother can say.

So now there is something new to be afraid of. Her body. *What is happening to me?* She must guard against the smell. She must be on the alert to find a household job to do when games are mentioned. The waiting, the alertness, exhaust her. She holds her arms tightly to her sides in company lest the slightest whiff should reach disgusted nostrils. Compulsively she washes her underarms, scrubbing with the washer, sniffing, scrubbing again. She pads them with hankies that she furtively changes throughout the day. Her body has become a loathsome thing that must be constantly watched lest it betray her.

'From now on you are to go to and from the bathroom fully clothed,' says Mummy.

'But the boys...'

'Never mind them. You are a girl and must be careful. It is not right, with young boys growing up in the house, that you are not fully clothed.'

Matti sits in her evening bath, tense and listening, afraid that the bathroom door will burst open and a small willie will waggle and splash a spray of yellow into the toilet bowl before her. And she in the bath, unclothed! *Keep away, please. Keep away. I'm nearly out. See, I'm dry. I'm dressed. I'm running to my room.*

Unbeknown to any of them, Mrs Milton has been praying for a miracle and the miracle has happened. She is torn with guilt that somehow she has caused this to happen by her wishing. She has miscarried the newcomer in a vile bloody episode of red and clots and hideous pains. She has paid for her wish with the pains of a childbirth that leaves her flat and exhausted and ill for weeks. And alone. For there is no one she can tell about her relief.

Finally when she is well enough to get up she goes to the church to talk to the priest. First she confesses her sins and he absolves her of any lingering stain that her relief might be causing. 'It was God's will, my child. You were prepared to carry out His will and hence no stain attaches to you. God knows what is best for each and every one of us. His will be done.' He prepares to dismiss her and she gathers all her courage.

'Father, there is something else.'

'Yes, my child.' Through the dark of the grille, she sees his head resting on his hands, the closed eyes, the nicotined fingers. 'What is it?'

'Father, there must be no more children. What am I to do about it?'

'My child, have I not told you, God in His infinite wisdom only sends to each of us what we can bear? Trust in God, my child, and all things are possible.'

'But Father,' she hears herself speak. She is astonished. Where has the courage come from? It is the desperation of despair. 'But Father, I know, I know I simply cannot have any more children. Father, does the Church permit me to end... to end relations... with my husband?'

'The Church looks upon relations between a husband and wife as a gift God has given them primarily for the procreation of children and secondarily as a means to enhance their marriage.'

'But Father, I do not want more children and these relations do not enhance anything for me. I want them to cease.'

'This is very difficult, my child. Could you not give it more thought before being so definite? Pray . . .'

'I have prayed.'

'Have you discussed this with your husband?'

'No.'

'Well, this must be done. The Church would only look with favour upon the ceasing of relations if both parties had agreed. After all, as a wife your duty to your husband is paramount. You cannot cease relations if it is against his will. Is that clear?'

'Yes, Father. Thank you, Father.' Mrs Milton rises and stumbles from the claustrophobic cubicle. Her heart is black with anger at him. How dare he? How dare he tell her what is best for husband and wife? How could he know? He has never had to submit like she has to the foul act of congress. She is goaded, strong with rebellion. For one short, proud moment in her life she will not submit. She returns home and tells her husband.

'There is to be no more of that business, Patrick.'

'What business?'

'In bed. There are to be no more children and the only way to prevent them is to end that business. No more.' She means it and he, shocked, sees a determination and hardness in her eyes that he has never seen before. Confronted, he must take her at her word.

ELEVEN

Matti is to start as a boarder at the Sacre Coeur. Desmond has been away with the Jesuits for a year now and in time all the little Miltons will become boarders. It will make men of them. Matti is no exception. Dr Milton has no illusions as to his childrearing habits. He's tough. He knows it and is proud of it. He knows no other way to be. He must take his model from his own upbringing. It has stood him in good stead. Where else would he have got the monumental discipline needed to conduct his life's work? It must be right. He cannot afford to have doubts. But before she goes he will try to capture his little sheila again, just the two of them, friends, working together. He misses his little sheila.

Dr Milton has taken up sketching. He has a set of HB pencils and some fine stiff sketching paper and he is applying himself to mastering the art. He sometimes thinks that if he is lacking in any area, it is in his knowledge of the arts. Medical school has let him down in this area. Although, of course, art for art's sake is nonsense. However, doing a little sketching will be a relaxation and an example to the family. He has, long ago, banned colouring books for the children. There is no skill in them, no creativity, and he would prefer the children not to waste their time on such rubbish. If they want to paint or draw freehand, he'll be only too willing to help. He hopes that, by example, they will see how pleasurable and constructive an occupation it can be.

Dr Milton particularly fancies the art of figure drawing, but he needs someone to pose for him. The little boys are too little. They cannot be expected to sit still for so long. Dr Milton will get Matti to pose for him. She won't get the chance once she goes away.

He goes to look for her. Matti is dreaming, mooning over a

record cover. He cannot help himself. He is displeased. It is only with the utmost difficulty that his wife has persuaded him that *The King and I* is lovely and can't do any harm. So he'd let the children go to the film and next thing you know the record is in the house and here is Matti, wasting time.

'What are you doing, dear?' Matti looks up, guilty.

'Nothing.'

'Matti!'

'I was looking at the picture, the dress, I think it's lovely. She's so pretty.'

'You know I don't like you sitting indoors on a lovely day like this. We're going up to the park.'

'What for?'

'I want to do some drawing and I want you to come with me. You can help.'

'But Daddy . . .'

'At once!'

Matti and her father set out for the park. They do not speak. She is sulky, resentful. He can tell. It is hot. She hates the blouse she is wearing. What if someone sees her? Can't Mummy see that it is too tight in the front, that she is bursting out of it? And what about the spots that have suddenly erupted on her back. Big blobs of pus. She can't help think about them. Dr Milton steps out briskly. No point in ambling along. No good walking unless you do it properly. His lips move. He is talking to himself, telling himself this as they go along.

When they reach the park they head down the hill, stumbling through the tussocks. They cross the cricket pitch, skirt the large pond and walk up the avenue of paperbarks. Here Dr Milton stops.

'This is the spot. Now what I want you to do, Matti, is to hop up into that tree there, that's the girl.' Matti climbs into the tree. 'No, stop there, turn around a bit, no, not so far, there, stop! Now look out over there towards the pavilion.' Matti looks out over there. For a moment. Then she turns back. 'No Matti. You have to stay quite still.' He busies himself preparing his pencils and paper. Matti shifts on the branch. 'Quite still!'

'But, Daddy, it's uncomfortable.'

'Matti!' A long time passes.

This is the most boring thing I have ever done. Surreptitiously she shifts from one buttock to the other. Out of the corner of her eye she observes her father. His tongue is protruding slightly. He is biting it. Concentrating.

'Now Matti, get down. I want to try it from another angle. I want to try it closer up. There. Sit just there. Head towards me. Put your legs over the... Dear, oh dear, you've got such big legs, Matti. Pity you got mine, not your mother's.'

I hope you mess up your stupid drawing and all your pencils break. Pig.

The afternoon drags on. Dr Milton will not do things by halves. He is determined to master this new skill and dusk is falling when he tells Matti to come down out of the tree.

'Well, my dear, what do you think?' He is pleased. Matti looks at the stilted, ridiculous drawings one by one. They're terrible. Can't he see that? 'Not bad for a first try, eh? Like anything, it is not mastered without practice. You've been a great help to your old Dad, Matti. Thank you.' Perhaps it has not been so bad. He is pleased with her. Has it really been so hard to earn his appreciation? No, not really. But she is tired, grubby, stiff. Earn it, earn it, earn it, that's what's wrong. Why has she got to *earn* it?

In the two weeks before Matti leaves to become a boarder it does seem that he is gentler, less demanding, more like her real Daddy. A surprising warmth, a sense of intimacy and unity seems to have invaded the house and she creeps within its orbit. This is exactly how Dr Milton has planned it, wants it to be.

Up they go to the park again. This time Daddy carries Little Brother on his shoulders and the other five are strung out in a line, keeping up the steady jogging pace that Daddy sets. When they arrive they follow their father to the flat land in the centre of the park, close to the formal rose garden. Dr Milton gathers them around him at the entrance to a dry stormwater drain and produces a bundle of firecrackers and some string from his coat.

'Here, Matti. You unwind this string for me. Quick. That's the girl. Now we'll tie the string onto the wicks of the bungers and the

Tom Thumbs to make them really long.' They stand watching as their father intently prepares the bundles of crackers he has brought. He is smiling a wide smile of anticipation.

'All right. Who wants to hear a really good bang, eh?'

'Me!'

'Me!'

'Me!'

'Stay where you are. I'll be back in a second.' The children hunker down at the entrance to the dried-out drain and watch as he disappears into the darkness. Little Brother begins to wail. 'I want my Daddy. I want my Daddy.'

'He'll be back in a sec,' says Matti, hoisting him up onto her hip. They peer into the drain.

'Here he comes! Here he comes!' And sure enough here comes Dr Milton in a crouching run, letting out the ball of string behind him. They jump about and clap their hands in excitement.

'Now, you chaps, I'm going to light the string and you're to run as fast as you can over to those trees when I say so.' They watch as he lights the match and protects the flame until the string has caught.

'Run!' Off they scamper, terrified and elated, and Dr Milton scoops up the two littlest and tucks them under his arms as they go. They gather in a huddle, hardly breathing and then it happens. BOOM. BOO-BOOM. BOOM. BOOM. The sound of the bungers echoes wave-like down the drain and Little Brother falls over backwards. Then off go the Tom Thumbs, a series of short, sharp gunshots of sound that leave them jumping and screaming in delight.

'Do it again, Daddy. Do it again.' But Dr Milton shakes his head.

'Once is enough,' he says, grinning hugely.

They are so excited they continue to leap about and start doing somersaults on the manicured lawns (Little Brother's all crooked so Matti has to grab his legs and lift him over).

'You do one, Daddy,' she yells. 'You do one.' So he does, and just as he goes over he breaks wind. The children stop in their tracks and look anxiously at their father, but he bursts out laughing and they all start for home shouting, 'Daddy made a rude noise. Daddy made a rude noise.' The Day of the Crackers they always call it afterwards, and they giggle at the memory of the most surprising cracker of them all.

It is that—and the nights on the top verandah—that Matti remembers before she goes away. Some nights Dr Milton lights the old black-out lamps and they sit in a huddle on the verandah and read *The Jungle Book*. Desmond and Matti sit on either side of their father.

'You be the narrator, Matti. Desmond, you read Mowgli tonight and I'll be Shere Khan the Tiger. And Mat, you read Little Grey Brother as well,' Dr Milton pulls Little Brother Milton onto his lap as he says it.

Other nights he gets them out of their beds very late.

'Come out onto the top verandah. Quiet now, little chap, so your mother doesn't hear us or it will be paddywhack on the drumstick.' And sleepy little fellows and their sister join him on the verandah while he tells them about the stars. It barely matters that Matti is not the one cuddled on his lap, feeling his fingers absently stroking her hair. Now it is Little Brother's turn and she crouches, wistful but warm at her father's feet, listening and loving him. His voice murmurs. He tells them and tests them.

'Tell me, Matti. What is that, over there, low in the sky?'

'Aldebaran, the Bull,' she shouts in triumph.

'Ssh. Ssh. Wooden spoon. Smacks. Ssh.'

Dr Milton draws in his breath in a delicious parody of fear and Matti hugs her legs tight against her chest and, oh yes, she is happy. She is happy.

'Now you, Little Brother. The planets please.' The tiny boy tenses himself on his father's lap.

'Mercuryvenusearthmarsjupitersaturnuranusneptunepluto.'

'Well done, little chap. What an excellent little chap. What a dear little chap.' Dr Milton's voice is warm and proud and full of boyish glee. Matti feels her heart will burst with love of him and love of Little Brother who can make Daddy so happy.

They all take their turn—Betelgeuse, Bellatrix, the Saucepan, the Belt, the Pointers to the Cross, the Cross itself. They listen to each other and the night breathing gently around them, and pad silently away when finally their father hoists Little Brother onto his shoulder and leaves to deposit him in his cot.

The day before she is to go, Matti and her mother are busy. They sit together sewing name tags on the singlets and stockings and suspender belts and underpants, on blouses and handkerchiefs and sheets and pillow cases and linen table napkins. Beside them on the floor are two new cases and a soft mohair rug.

Suddenly her mother puts down her sewing and looks at Matti. She picks awkwardly at the cloth of the chair. She clears her voice. Matti looks at her in surprise. She feels a prickle of uncertainty. She looks keenly at her mother and thinks how beautiful she is. Matti wishes she had blue eyes like her mother and those shadowy depressions beneath her high cheek bones. Her mother looks anxious. The prickle deepens.

'Matti, there are some things you have to know. Have you heard of your . . . your menses?' Matti looks at her mother and feels herself flush. Something about herself that is not nice, not at all nice, is coming. Her mother looks wretched and uncomfortable. So too, now, is Matti.

'No, Mummy. My what?'

'You will have noticed changes . . . um . . . your armpits . . .' Matti feels herself redden. The smell. 'Well, blood will come from down here . . .' her mother gestures, 'every month and you will wear a pad to soak it up. You must be very clean.' Matti stares at her in astonishment. 'Do you have any questions?'

'Oh I . . .' She can't really believe what she has heard. 'Oh. Every month?'

'Isn't that enough?' Her mother sounds angry.

'But why? Why does it happen!' Now her mother sounds angry still, but exhausted too.

'You'll find that out soon enough. I'll get you some pads and a belt from the chemist tomorrow. Make sure you pack them.' Abruptly she stands and leaves the room. Matti sits. She is horrified by what she has just heard. Maybe if she doesn't think about it, Mummy will forget and the whole unbelievable thing will go away.

But Mummy does not forget. The next day Matti finds a fat brown paper bag on her bed that crackles loudly when she pokes it and an elastic belt with safety pins. She puts them quickly into the bottom of her case and pretends they aren't there. Then she takes the school requirement list and item by item she places them in the case, ticking them off as she goes. Her mother enters to supervise the last of the packing.

'Well, Matti, I know you are going to be a good girl and work hard for Daddy and me and get to wear a Blue Ribbon of Excellence in your final year. Never forget, Matti, that your family will be the only ones through life who will really stand by you so you must pay us back by being a credit to us.'

'Oh, I will, Mummy, I will.' She is terribly excited to be off.

'Oh, Matti. One more thing. You're growing up now. It's time you stopped calling me Mummy. You should call me Mother from now on.' Matti stares at her. She will never call her anything again.

Matti dresses and carries her cases proudly downstairs. Her mother is on the phone. She indicates with a gesture where Matti is to place her things. Then she hangs up. 'Aunty Kath will pick you up in half an hour. They are driving Colleen back.'

Matti does not immediately understand. They are relatives she barely knows, their daughter five years older than she. A twinge of hurt threatens to spoil her excitement and pride. She had imagined them all piling into the old car and she would nurse Little Brother and they would deliver her in triumph to the school and kiss her and hug her and maybe even cry because they would miss her so much, like in books. She pushes down the disappointment.

'That was Daddy on the phone then. He's been held up with an urgent. As soon as he gets in we have to take Desmond back.'

Matti nods.

I hate Desmond. I hate you and most of all I hate him.

Her aunt pulls up and Matti and her mother, who have been waiting at the gate, kiss each other goodbye. Matti climbs into the car. She turns to wave out the back window but, already, the gate is shut. That world is closed neatly off. In an impersonal and kindly way her relatives deposit her in the midst of two hundred milling girls and a welter of cases. Matti is back. She belongs here. The attendants of her brain, fear and anxiety and tension, lift and bow before her and back silently out of her mind. Matti is at home, at ease. *Oh yes, I am happy. So happy. Happy. Happy. Happy.*

TWELVE

There was no sound in the hospital room except the hum of the drip and the sound of her father's heavy breathing. Margaret stretched and adjusted the rug that was slipping from her lap. Was it true? That the painful memories no longer moved her to anger or hate or revenge. Merely a weariness and above all a deep sadness that she would carry them, anaesthetised by scar tissue though they were, for the rest of her life. The imprints were too deep to obliterate. They were her heritage, for better or worse.

'Comfortable, are you?' asked Sister, coming in on her rounds. Margaret looked up. She glanced at her father. His breathing was fairly quiet.

'Yes,' she whispered.

'We're going to turn him. He's wasted and it's very sore for him if he lies in the same spot for too long. See?' The nurse held up one of the arms. At the elbow Margaret could see the reddish spots that threatened to bruise the tired flesh.

'Can I help?' she asked. The nurse nodded and Margaret moved to the bedside. Her father opened his eyes as they turned him lightly and adjusted the pillows under his legs and arms.

'Thank you, my dear, thank you,' he murmured. Margaret caught her breath at the memory. Hadn't he always been courteous? There was not one family meal she could recall where he had not uttered his thanks to her mother at the conclusion of it. 'Thank you, my dear, thank you.' She brushed away hot tears at the waste of it all. The nurse brought her tea and left the two of them alone.

'Sleeping were you, dear?' her father asked.

'No, I wasn't, Daddy. Just sitting here, thinking.' She rushed on. 'About the past. You and me, and everything and...' He was gesturing towards the water glass. She held the bent straw to his dry lips and he sucked a drop. The moment had passed. But she had to try.

'All these years you've been sick, Daddy, I suppose you've had plenty of time to think.'

'Indeed I have, my dear.'

'Any regrets?' Oh, how shamelessly she was digging.

'Not really. Perhaps one. I regret that I could not get your mother to travel with me when I was studying in England. I begged her to. I was very lonely. She wouldn't. I regret that. But, she had to look after you little ones, you and Desmond. She's been a wonderful mother to you, Matti. An example. I wish, my dear, I wish... that you and your mother got on together.' He said it in a rush. He was watching her.

'I know, Daddy. I know.' Whatever she said would be totally inadequate, and what difference could it make to him now? But she was unable to lie.

'I don't think she likes me, really. She believes there is one way of doing things but I don't do things her way... I...' But his eyes had lost their light. Their few words had tired him. Margaret rubbed a little vaseline onto his lips and adjusted the bedclothes up under his chin. As she did so, he fumbled to the side, his hand searching. She took the old hand in her own and held it tight. He sighed and returned to whatever world a dying man inhabits.

When his grip relaxed she left the bedside and moved over to the photos on the shelf. That of her mother showed a young woman with huge, light-filled eyes, looking up at something out of camera range. It was impossible to look at the face without sensing the anticipation and excitement therein. It was the picture of a young woman certain of the marvellous potential of her life.

Margaret took it off the shelf and carried it to her chair beside the window. She sat down again and laid the photo on her lap. Slowly, with her index finger, she traced the lovely young face, curving her hand over the glossy swept-back hair, lingering over the contours of the high cheek bones, over the slim nose and round the jaw with its proud sure uplift facing the years to come with confidence.

'Look me in the eye,' she whispered, and tried to give her mother a name, but that had been lost many years before. 'Look me in the eye and believe that I am sorry it's not been as you had hoped. Believe me if I tell you I am sorry for the part I've played in your unhappiness. Believe me when I say that none of it was done deliberately to hurt you.' She was crying. Tears had fallen on the face she held in her lap. 'I've needed a mother so often. I've tried to make up for it by adopting mothers over the years. But they weren't you. My birth mother.' She dashed her fist across her eyes and dried the tears. She grabbed the hem of her shirt and wiped the frame. 'What did you adopt, to make up for me? Did you get the closeness you needed? I might be different from you in lots of ways but surely we both need the same things? Acknowledgement, love, affirmation of a job well done. Even if you could like me a little bit, I'd be glad.' Her father made a sudden snorting sound and she looked over to him, cradling the cold glass of her mother's photo against her hot cheek. 'We know so little about each other,' she whispered across the silent room.

THIRTEEN

Oh, it's good to be back! The humid stillness of the February air hangs over the convent but, within, the sandstone gives off the damp coolness that Matti knows so well. She stands in Queen's Square, a wide hallway outside the study room. Towering over the cases and the panamas is a huge, plaster statue of the Queen of Heaven. The air is alive for a short while with shrieks of recognition and excited chatter. On the blackboard are long lists of instructions. They are written in the flowing, stylised hand that is known and recognised all over the world (so they have been told) as Sacre Coeur writing. Very soon Matti will be attending Saturday evening classes in which they will strive to emulate the hand. They will be dealt slope cards with immaculate examples, ink wells and special dip nibs. Not one of them will be permitted to use a fountain pen until she has mastered the style with precision.

She scans the strange faces, subdued but undaunted. She looks for Flynn, her link with the past. She'll be along presently (but probably late, because only now is she getting round to tossing things into her case on her bedroom floor).

A bell starts to ring, urgently and querulously. The chatter dies slowly and the girls stand uncertainly. 'You are to move off, class by class, as you are called,' announces a nun. 'The order, therefore, will be most junior to most senior. That is, fourth, third, second, first and finally upper first. Would the fourth class now make their way down the corridor to the left and wait at the foot of the Tower Stairs which they will find at the end.' Down they go, an untidy scramble of girls and at the foot of the Tower Stairs a tiny nun, almost a dwarf nun, beckons to them.

'Good evening, children.' There is a muttered response. 'When I say "Good evening, children," you will reply, "Good evening, Mother." So, "Good evening, children.'"

'Good evening, Mother.'

'My name is Mother Porter. I am the fourth class mistress. Please form two orderly ranks as quickly as possible.' The girls mill about. 'Very good. Follow me quietly.' Mother Porter moves to the head of the ranks and climbs briskly and purposefully up the stairs, the girls surging behind. Half way up the second flight she stops and turns to face them. The girls pile up, push forward, collide with the people in front of them. For a moment Mother Porter waits, very still, and they too settle and fall still. 'These are the Tower Stairs. These are your stairs. You will learn to move up and down them like ladies and next year, when you are older and, I hope, more responsible, you will be permitted to use the main staircase with the rest of the school. Speaking is never permitted on the Tower Stairs. Speaking is never permitted in any of the school corridors or in any of the bathrooms. When we move up and down the stairs, the leader of the ranks will stop at the end of each flight. When you hear my signal,' she raises her hand to indicate the little wooden clapper in her palm, 'you will move off again. There will never be any need for talking.' She turns again and snaps the signal. Off they move. Up and up, three more floors, their feet clumping on the smooth, worn, wooden boards. Then they move out onto a landing, the girls in the rear straining to see what is ahead of them.

'Now children, here we are. This is the Holy Family dormitory. Speaking is never permitted in the dormitory. As I read out your name, please move into the alcove designated to you.' In a clear, light voice, she calls their names. Matti looks around in delight. In her overnight stays as a junior she has slept in the infirmary and has never seen this part of the school. The dormitory is divided into alcoves by pink and white and green floral curtains and the roof slopes all the way to the floor on the far side. Along that side the windows open to the harbour, winking, blinking, far away.

Each little alcove contains a spartan-looking iron bedstead and a horsehair mattress, a pile of linen waiting folded at its end. Beside the bed is a wooden locker and a chair. That is all. Clack, clack, clack.

'Please make your beds at once, children. On Saturday we will have a bed-making lesson so you can learn to make your beds correctly. This evening, however, just do them as quickly and quietly as possible. Your cases are waiting at the end of the dormitory. Take from them what you need for tonight and tomorrow you will take anything extra to the linen room and your cases to storage in the loft.'

A bustle of activity breaks out in the alcoves. Clack, clack, clack goes the signal.

'Your chairs are never for sitting on, children. You will place them outside your alcove each night. On them you will place your folded bedspread, then your underclothing and over the top you will drape your uniform. Your shoes will be placed under your chair. Make sure to close your curtains when you are undressing and leave them closed when you are in bed. Sacred Heart of Jesus, Immaculate Heart of Mary.' The girls start to shuffle about again. Clack, clack, clack. 'When I say, "Sacred Heart of Jesus, Immaculate Heart of Mary," you will reply, "I give you my heart." So, Sacred Heart of Jesus, Immaculate Heart of Mary.'

'I give you my heart,' they chorus. Matti glances around. Everyone is tentative, perhaps nervous. No one is banging or coughing or exchanging glances. She looks at her neighbour, a slight girl with large glasses.

'Hello,' whispers Matti. The girl looks startled, glancing in the direction of Mother Porter.

'Hello,' she whispers back. She is unpacking her pyjamas.

'What's on your pyjamas?' asks Matti curiously. They are very cheerful. 'Gollywogs, are they!'

'No,' replies the other indignantly. 'It's the Olympic Games.'

'Oh,' says Matti. She turns back to her unpacking but a gentle tap on the shoulder makes her jump.

'Margaret-Anne. I thought I made it clear. There is to be no talking in the dormitory. I am disappointed. Remember, as one of our juniors, so much more is expected of you.'

'Sorry, Mother.'

Clack, clack, clack.

'In five minutes we will move to the basin rooms. Everyone is to wear her dressing gown and slippers and bring her face towel and toilet bag. Talking is not permitted in the basin rooms. Showers are taken each morning before Mass and tomorrow you will be allocated a night for your weekly bath. Head-washing only takes place on Saturday morning. No child is to wash her hair at any other time. No child is to wash any article of clothing. Bags for soiled clothes will be placed in the dormitory twice a week. Hurry now, and when you hear my signal, move quietly into ranks at the dormitory door.'

'Hello, Matti. Where were you? I've been hanging around downstairs looking.'

'Flynn!' snaps Mother Porter. 'You will enter the dormitory in silence please. By your lateness you have missed out on a great deal of important information. Come over here to me and I will run through it for your benefit. And remember, complete silence!'

Matti hurries to undress and finish storing her belongings. Carefully she lifts out the brown paper parcel that lies at the bottom of her case. It crackles as she touches it. She freezes, breathing hard. Quickly, furtively, she shoves it to the back of her cupboard. When will it happen? Will she really ever need such a thing?

Then, hearing Mother Porter's signal, she parts the curtains and joins the ranks. Within fifteen minutes they have filed back down the Tower Stairs, washed and cleaned their teeth and returned to the long room under the eaves. Matti does not feel the slightest bit lonely as she hops into bed. She loves it. Everything so organised and matter-of-fact and clear. Rules, blessed understandable rules. No confusion, no tension. She lies still and watches in a detached, puzzled way as an arm shoots through the curtain waving a small jar with a sponge in it. In a moment a head follows. Mother Porter.

'When I offer you the holy water, you sit up and bless yourself and say, "Good night and God bless you, Mother."' Matti sits up, stabs her finger into the jar and blesses herself.

'Good night and God bless you, Mother.'

'Good night and God bless you, Margaret-Anne.' And suddenly

Mother Porter smiles. 'Sleep well, my dear. It is so nice to have you here with us.'

Oh yes. Happy. Happier. Happiest ever.

In barely a week the girls are used to the routine: to the great bell that clangs raucously at six a.m. to rouse them; to the more mellow bell that tolls solemnly as they file to the chapel; to the meal bells and the class bells and the recreation bells; to the impatient ding ding ding bell that hurries out a code for nuns who are urgently needed elsewhere; to the bell that announces a solemn warning at nine p.m. that the Grand Silence has fallen.

The long ranks file from the dining room after afternoon tea, They have drunk sweet, milky tea from huge enamel teapots, gobbled the weekly treat of sticky pink iced buns and are moving past the piano cells to change for sport. At the door of the changing room, the ranks come to an untidy halt. Scuffle and murmur gradually subside. This is what Mother Porter, on recreation duty, has been waiting for. Then they must wait a further five minutes to discipline themselves and reflect upon their disorderly approach. Finally, they are permitted through the door. Mother Porter, too small to supervise properly in the huge, draughty room, climbs without embarrassment onto the bench that runs around the wall.

She watches them. The older, more confident girls remove their uniforms without concern and slip on their sports tunics. The younger, shyer ones, try to fit behind the tunic rack to change in privacy. Matti is among them. She still wears her childish, immature singlet and longs for, feels ashamed without, a bra. Mother Porter sees it all. She smells the smell of over a hundred girls. The rank smell of armpits, the odour of stale menstrual blood, the sweetish cloy of baby powder, the stiff, biscuity smell of soiled stockings. She finds this time of day trying, a penance. She sighs to herself and knows she must shortly deliver her yearly lecture to her fourth class charges. They are the most likely offenders in the area of personal freshness. Mother Porter still finds it surprising that so many of her charges come to her so unprepared for the onset of womanhood. Some girls, she knows, will even try to avoid hair-washing at times and tell her stuff and nonsense about wet hair and periods. Mother Porter will brook no such twaddle. Soon she will have them sorted out.

Now she signals that they may pull back the bolts and open the heavy doors to the exterior. Out they file, skirting the gardens and lawns, through the tunnel, up the steps past the cotoneaster and lantana and morning glory and onto the playing fields. Once more Mother Porter waits for order and signals for the prayers to start. 'Our Father', 'Hail Mary', 'Glory Be'. It ends. She rings the recreation bell and the games begin.

Matti has been allotted a fielder job in the out-field. She definitely dislikes sport. Mens sana. Out here, away from much likely action she can moon about and dream and not do much at all. And her possie near the high bank means she can look for four-leaf clovers. Recreation was more fun in Junior School when they could run about with friends and walk in pairs or sit in Cocky's Cage, the little green-painted summer-house in the centre of the fields and listen to Mother reading a story book. Now that they are seniors it is strictly forbidden to walk in pairs or have special friendships. Matti hardly ever gets a chance to talk to Flynn who is sitting, bold as brass, on the wooden wall of Cocky's Cage, swinging her legs and weaving a chain of clover flowers. Matti is tempted to desert her post and go and join her but she does not. Matti obeys the rules. Still, she admires Flynn. Here comes Mother Porter, waving her finger and shaking her head and Matti sees Flynn slip casually from the wall and amble away, fixing her chain in her hair meanwhile.

Matti sees Mother Porter make a notation in her notebook. This will be consulted when she is deciding the Weekly Notes. Each week Reverend Mother hands out small cards at a formal meeting in the hall which state, 'very good', 'good', 'fair', 'unsatis-factory'. Matti intends to get 'very good' or at the worst 'good' during her boarding days. After all, 'fair' will mean not being permitted to go on a home visit on a Sunday and Matti has no intention of that! Oh, she'd be perfectly happy to stay at school all the time but Daddy will take a very dim view of 'fair' and want to know the reason why. Matti is going to keep Daddy out of school affairs at all costs. Yet there's Flynn. Risking her Weekly Note every day of her life. Uncaring. How Matti envies her.

The ranks file into the dining room which, even on summer nights when the doors to the outside are left open to catch the harbour breeze, smells of mashed potato and old boiled things. The girls move to their tables, one girl from each class, to discourage special friendships, and stand behind their chairs until the grace bell is rung. 'Amen' they chorus, loudly, hungrily, and drag their chairs back with a deafening roar. The meal proceeds. It is steak today. Contorted grey hunks of meat, turning whitish with congealing fat. They must all have a portion. And they do. After all Mother Anton is on surveillance, prowling up and down the dining room, watching everybody, everything. There she goes, digging her finger into slumping backbones, tapping an elbow, indicating a fallen serviette. And all the time, as she walks, her hands move automatically, slitting open the envelopes she carries. No letter comes into the school whose contents she does not scan. Mother Anton is a remote and shadowy and severe figure to most of them. She is Mistress of Discipline and a summons to Mother Anton's office can only mean serious trouble and desperate examination of conscience. She is also the upper first mistress and these older girls speak glowingly of the nun, but only they.

The fourth class go up the Tower Stairs, out onto the landing and into their classroom, Blessed Phillipine, to prepare for class. Their mistress, Mother Porter, leaves them with their subject teacher and goes to her study. This is a tiny cubby-hole of a place and inside it Mother Porter roosts like a dumpy mother-hen. She collects her notes from her *pochon* and sits down to write up her weekly report. Short and dumpy she may be but with distractingly elegant hands, with long tapering fingers and perfect oval nails.

Having written her weekly report, she gathers her voluminous skirt in one hand and her files in the other and prepares to climb the stairs to the weekly teachers' meeting over which she will preside, while the spiritual, academic and disciplinary progress of her fourth class is discussed. Today it will be a short meeting.

'I would like to ask your comments on Flynn O'Brien. As far as I am concerned, she is undisciplined, sloppy and untidy in dormitory and lessons. Reports from Junior School indicate that she has an excellent brain and is capable of good work. She is not progressing at present to her full potential.'

'Flynn is going to be a great asset in choir,' says the singing mistress. 'She sings like an angel.'

'I am so glad to hear that,' says Mother Porter with an edge to her voice. 'I would be happier though if she confined her singing to choir and chapel. She sings in the corridors and on the Tower Stairs. Yesterday I had occasion to reprimand her for singing behind the closed door of the toilet.'

'Yes, Mother.'

'And it has been brought to my attention that she was playing chess under the desk with Margaret-Anne. They have been separated.' The other nuns nod. 'Now this.' Mother Porter delves deep into her habit. 'Only this morning, when I was going through Flynn's desk, I came across her Christian Doctrine book. As you can see, she has covered the margins with ridiculous drawings. Babies in nappies!' The nuns cluck among themselves.

Mother Porter returns the offending book to her pocket. Ridiculous but excellent, she thinks, but naturally she does not smile. 'Now are there any further adverse comments to be made?' A murmur here, a tug at the chin of the bonnet there, a flicker of movement of joined hands under the cape. 'No? Very well then.' Now she reads out the roll and enters the Weekly Note for each child. There is no superficial chatter. It is business-like and brisk and as the bell rings to signal the end of class, she stands and dismisses her colleagues.

'Thank you, Mothers,' she says and they all bow and take their leave.

FOURTEEN

Alone now, she turns her attention to the notes she has made concerning this term's entertainment. Mother Porter is in charge of the dramatic art. Dramatics has an honoured position in the traditions of the Order and she is the most capable person to maintain the standards. In consultation with Reverend Mother, she chooses the plays, advises on casting, organises and supervises rehearsals. She makes many of the costumes and attends to the technical aspects of lighting, set-painting and prop-making. She commandeers the art students to help her, describing, exhorting, nagging, flicking through books to illustrate and explain herself. As often as time permits she too grabs a paint brush, to create magical illusions on backdrops. With a mouthful of pins, a picture to guide her in accuracy and imagination, she seeks to achieve the look of a period with mere scraps of material. Her habit becomes dusty from the props, paint-stained, awry. She pins her veil back firmly for greater ease. Every night she has to dab and rub her black habit. It must be spotless for tomorrow. But it is at these times that energy and excitement flow from her and infect all those about her.

Mother Porter writes up a list on the Queen's Square blackboard and to her delight Matti has seen her name there. She is to present herself in the Hall directly after night prayers. Night prayers seem endless. Rosary, litany, special intentions, new hymns. She fidgets with her black veil, worries the holes in her gloves, shifts uncomfortably from knee to knee, bumpy, 'holy' knees. Her responses are scant, her attention perfunctory. As soon as it is over she replaces her veil in the veil cupboard and hurries to the Hall.

Others are there before her, standing in excited groups, talking quietly, unsure of what is to follow. In a few minutes Mother Porter toddles around the corner. She pulls the curtains of the foyer together firmly, makes a speedy circuit of the hall, switching on some lights, turning off others and, finally, calls the girls together in front of her.

'Go and sit on the stage steps please children. Everyone here?' She reads the roll then continues. 'This year for the Entertainment we are going to do *Antigone*.' The girls gasp in excitement. 'I'm sure I don't have to tell you that perfect behaviour is expected from each and every one of you. Failure in self-discipline will mean instant dismissal from the play. Is that clear?' The girls nod. 'Make the most of this opportunity offered you. The senior girls will become involved a little later on. Meanwhile, you younger ones will form the chorus.'

Mother Porter clears her throat. She has a little quiver of doubt as to what is to follow. Reverend Mother has discussed the play with her and suggested that it is a good opportunity for the younger girls to do a little eurhythmics between acts. So graceful, and Miss Duncan such a nice — unfortunate but nice — woman. Reverend Mother has heard from a dear friend 'outside' that Miss Duncan needs encouragement. And so she shall have it.

Mother Porter lifts her fob watch from under her cape and looks at it. Any minute now Miss Duncan will be upon them. Mother Porter scans the expectant faces. Shall she say anything? She decides not. She motions them to rise and just at that moment the foyer curtains are flung apart and a small figure launches herself into the hall in a crouching glide, trailing purple chiffon behind her. Bare feet patter on the parquet floor. Round the Hall speeds Miss Duncan, arms fluttering, back curved, sudden leaps and mouse-like squeaks. And then she stops, arms triumphantly aloft, head thrown back. Motionless.

The watching girls squirm uneasily. They look to Mother Porter for guidance. Her nostrils are twitching. Quickly. Firm action is needed. With a slight inclination of her head, she lifts her hands from under her cape and begins to clap. Ah. The blessed relief of

it. The girls clap as they have never clapped before. Hysteria
looms. Marie-Christine whistles. Mother Porter's head turns like a
whip-lash. Click, click, click goes the signal. Her finger indicates.
Marie-Christine creeps from the hall. Order is restored.

Miss Duncan's motionless figure stirs into life.

'Thank you, darlings. Now we shall all dance. Dance with me,
dance with me.' And she starts to skip recklessly round and round
again. The watching girls are frozen with embarrassment, their
eyes imploring towards Mother Porter.

Mother Porter moves to the steps.

'Quickly now. Shoes and socks off,' she whispers hoarsely. 'Miss
Duncan is here at Reverend Mother's express request.' One then
two, then, what the heck, down they step, throwing caution to
the wind. The Hall is a turmoil of follow-the-leader behind the
purple dress.

'Come now, darlings. Skip and crouch and curve the arms and
sigh the shoulders, sigh them, sigh them. And free and arch and
raise and smile and bend and down and heavy and heavy and slow
and creep and creep and curl and curl and slow and slow and
sleep.' So she croons and the room becomes very still. They rest,
motionless, and then Miss Duncan hops up, sprightly and lightly.

'And now we talk.' The girls sit up, laughter gone, interest and
relaxation making them beautiful and lithe. Miss Duncan explains
her plan, her ancient wrinkled face, the eyes behind the thick
lenses, alive and vital. 'We are going to dance between the acts. It
is important that we do not destroy the mood of the play, as I'm
sure Mother Porter would agree.' Mother Porter inclines her head
gratefully. 'Therefore, I want us to create a Greek frieze. We are
going to be decorations on the temple. We will be maidens and
athletes in frozen poses and we are going to move like a gentle
song from pose to pose, flowing like water from one attitude to
another. You, you will have the javelin and you the discus, and
you will be binding the victor's filet in your hair, and you will be
adjusting your tunic and you will be a runner and you will be
holding the torch aloft, and so we will go, thus...' And she rises
and demonstrates the movements and Mother Porter, sitting
quietly at the side, sees the frieze of the temple come alive.

Night after night they are drilled until their movements are as fluid and easy as a film dissolve. Miss Duncan in her flowing, colourful chiffon and glasses like the bottom of a tumbler has enchanted them, taken them back to ancient Greece and they are willing and able to stay there for the duration. But now she is no longer needed and rehearsals for the play itself get under way.

Mother Porter hands out the scripts. 'I do not like rehearsing children who are carrying scripts,' she says. 'One week from today I expect you all, with the possible exception of Antigone, Ismene and Creon, to be word-perfect.' Matti flicks through the thick, roneoed script. In two days she has learnt her lines and before the play opens she has learned all the other lines as well. Just in case.

Being in the play is hard work and Mother Porter continues to insist on absolute silence. When the Chorus is not on stage Matti curls up in a dusty corner of the wings, covers herself with a sheet of canvas, and watches, mouthing the words as the older girls go through the timeless tragedy of *Antigone*. No longer just an onlooker, she has become part of the process. She is lost in the magic of the experience, the smell of the dusty drops, the harsh glare of the lights with the dust motes floating thickly in their beams, the mystery of the darkness out beyond the footlights. More than anything else it is the warmth that she loves, and its enveloping, heavy, comfort.

Now she is curled up, watching. How she envies the older girls, their hair upswept, ribbons twining through, their silky tunics, coloured cords crossing their breasts. Matti hugs her chest and wishes for breasts. If once in a while one of these girls acknowledges her in any way, Matti shivers, thrilled.

All her waking hours are now directed to what they do in the Hall. The lucky cast are drawn further and further from the mainstream of school life. They are sent to early supper so that they will have longer rehearsal time before the falling of the Grand Silence. At these unsupervised meals they may sit with whomever they please. They are ordered to take Second Rises, lest they get too tired, so morning after morning, they lie in bed and listen as the rest of the school dresses and files down to Mass. Only then do they have to rise and slowly, luxuriously, they can shower in empty bathrooms before joining the others at breakfast. Afternoon recreation time is used for rehearsals and from the windows of the

Hall, Matti can see the ranks filing out to the fields. She draws up her shoulders and breathes deeply. She has found her enchanted place.

And then the play is over. The feelings, the memories, the warmth she hugs close to herself, reliving the magic, to feed on until next time.

FIFTEEN

Margaret stood still, her head resting on the window pane, staring into the darkness outside the hospital. She was full of gratitude to the nuns who had given her the first taste of what had become her life's work. Not as early as she had intended but... eventually.

The Hampstead theatre and those in Birmingham, Liverpool, Manchester, Durham, the summer performances in the Lakes District, seemed so far away from the hospital room and this dying man. Her days of research in the National Library and the British Museum and the galleries, lay in the distance like glorious sunbursts of contentment. She smiled to herself as she thought of the early days, fifteen years ago, and of her first 'character', Caroline Lamb, her uncertainty as to whether she could research adequately, write a script with conviction, and, most important of all, whether she could turn all that into a real person on stage. Those hard early days as she did the rounds of agents trying to convince them that, indeed, she could tackle the performance herself. That a small injection of funds was all she needed from a backer — and a tiny stage. She thought with gratitude of her women friends who had finally put up the money, encouraging her, trusting her, until reviews came out and the theatres started to fill. She thought of her daughters who had heard her lines over and over again until it was as if another person had joined their household. She thought of times when she had been snappy and sharp with anxiety or weariness and how her children had left her to herself until the crisis was past. There had been four 'guests' in their lives now, Caroline, then Isobel Burton, then Virginia Woolf, her favourite, and now, just about ready to present to the public, Gwen John, of the calm, melancholy, exquisite paintings that she had visited day after day, sinking into the knowledge of the determined woman behind their creation.

Would she have done it if she and Robert had not grown tired of a marriage littered with battles? She knew that she would not have. There had simply not been a scrap of energy left over from the exhaustion of the little ones and his need for a compliant, passive wife who would take over where his mother had left off, permitting him to come home to a tidy house, a tidy wife and well-cooked meals for his friends most Friday nights. She remembered how her English mother-in-law had said, when they announced the divorce, 'The trouble with you arty young women is you don't want to pick up the underpants.' She had hooted with laughter. It was quite true.

And she was much happier when the underpants were not even an issue. After a bitter year of separation in which she had accused Robert aloud of being just like her father, trying to control and manipulate her so that she no longer knew where her feelings lay, and accused him silently of letting her down just as her father had, not loving her enough, not making her the shining star in his firmament, she had retired, exhausted from the pain they were inflicting on each other, and had decided to let him be. At once the change had come. Robert had let her be also and they were able to meet on territory of vital and mutual importance — their children. Robert had never let the children down on visiting arrangements or holiday plans. He had always been available to take their phone calls and listen to their concerns or their triumphs. They had managed to negotiate successfully on the only but also the most important remnant of their marriage. She was proud of that. And her own special work had begun.

She turned from the window and walked back to the bedside. A harsh rasping sound came from her father's slightly open mouth. You did what you could then, after the divorce, didn't you? The cheques that came each year, with the little note, 'To help with the children', that I never once even acknowledged. I thought they were my due. *Oh, Daddy.* She put her hand on his head trying to transmit the compassion that she felt.

I am my father's daughter. I too am tough. I did not let go, despite the blood and the mutilation and death's hand in mine, urging me to drown in the freezing waters of total confusion and despair.

SIXTEEN

It is late in the winter term. The Gothic starkness, the windows rattling in their ill-fitting frames, the wind whistling and howling around the towers and corners and up the stairwells exacerbate the Sydney winter. The girls believe the convent is the coldest place in the world. Girls and nuns suffer together. Chilblains inflame and crust on blueish fingers, noses are red and dripping. Showers in the freezing bathrooms are a penance. Girls wear jumpers over and under their tunics. Some of the nuns wear black cardigans under their capes. Only the Mistress of Discipline makes a virtue of suffering. She selects a team of marchers, the Spartans, who drill every morning to martial music on the flat roof, across which the wind sweeps unhindered. She expects her Spartans to eschew jumpers and mittens and 'offer it up'. It is a small, select group. Despite mens sana, Matti is not among them.

Winter term is always a trial for the nuns. Wind seems to unsettle the girls. Discipline is harder to implement. They are restless. They tend to shriek. They are sluggish preparing for morning Mass. They are slow over breakfast. They nurse their cups of tea. They are scatty.

Nevertheless, for Matti, the winter term holds romance. She imagines that in secret places of the great building, dramas, tragedies, heroics are possible. Like Northanger Abbey, or Manderley or Mr Rochester's West Wing. The mood, the gloom, the eeriness excite her imagination. She sees the building as a huge stage set and she waits, in excited anticipation, for the drama to unfold.

As occasionally it does. Which is another reason she loves the

Sacre Coeur so much. Each Saturday night, the fourth class gathers for a meeting with Mother Porter. It is the most intimate time of the school week as they sit listening, radiators glowing in recognition of the occasion. They darn their stockings with the aid of wooden darning mushrooms and look forward to the story that Mother Porter will presently read to them, aware already that she will stop at a critical moment, leaving them with a cliff-hanger until next week.

Tonight, Mother Porter finishes the news and says: 'There will be no storybook tonight. Instead Mother Frisby is coming to see you.' The girls look at each other and murmur. Mother Frisby? She is an old nun, and they have seen her talking to herself. They have been told that she spent the war years in Japan and has been unwell ever since. She has been heard to tell noisy girls that little Japanese children are much better behaved.

Mother Porter signals and they stand to greet the old lady. She hobbles in leaning on a huge wooden staff. Mother Porter gives the customary bow and leaves the room.

'Quickly children,' says the old nun and they have to strain to catch her words. 'Push your desks back and pull your chairs into a circle. We're going to do some mind-reading.' Mind reading! They form a circle. From under her capacious black apron, Mother Frisby produces a lantern. With trembly old fingers she adjusts the mantle, lights the wick and as the flame grows into a flickering light she turns off the electricity. The girls sit very still, watching the ancient, wizened face in the gloom. The noise of the wind seems to pick up, an incessant howling.

'Are you all ready? What we are going to do is pick one of the group as our . . . let's call it subject. We must each remain very still and silent and on no account give away the person's name by glance or word. When we have each locked the name away inside ourselves I will open the door and invite a stranger in who will be able, after a short time, to guess the name of our subject. Are we ready? Who's it to be?'

'Me please, Mother.'

'Please, Mother, me.'

'Please, Mother.'

'Please, Mother.'

They wave their arms to catch her attention. She looks about her slowly, seriously.

'You, Denise. You will be first.'

They groan in disappointment.

'Never mind, you may be picked next time. We have plenty of time.' With extraordinary strength she pounds her staff on the floor and the door slowly opens. A figure totally enveloped in a black cloak enters, glides silently around the circle and then sits huddled in the centre. There is no way of knowing who it is, although it is clearly some nun, and she has a black veil hanging down both her back and over her face, concealing her identity. The girls murmur. Thump, thump, thump, goes the staff. 'Don't make a sound, children.' Thump, thump, thump. 'Even a cough or sniff could aid the stranger.' Thump, thump, thump-thump-thump. The stranger stirs. 'Not yet, my friend.' Thump. Thump. 'Stay still a little longer.' Thump. 'Even if you are ready, spend another few moments making quite sure.' A veritable roll and crash of the staff on the bare boards. The stranger rises from the huddle, picks up the lantern and glides to the blackboard. Holding the lantern aloft so that they can see clearly, the person spells out in large, firm letters, DENISE, places the lantern on the floor and glides from the room. The girls buzz with chatter. How did she guess? 'It's that noise, Mother. You're telling her with that thumping.'

'Do you think so, dear? Let us try again.' And again and again they play, wriggling and interrupting after each episode, but they can find no pattern to the noise that the old nun makes with her staff. Then, as suddenly as she arrived, Mother Frisby leaves, hobbling with her lantern from the room. For a minute they sit in total darkness, silent, unsure what to expect, hearing the windows rattle in their frames and the wind singing its discords in the chimneys. Then the lights come on in a sudden shocking glare and Mother Porter bustles in.

'Chairs and desks back, children. No talking please. Already it is late. Take your gloves and veils for morning Mass and go silently to the dormitory.'

Stunned, still half held in the other, dark and crashing world, they ready themselves and trudge up the Tower Stairs to bed.

This is Matti's chosen home. Her place of mystery and magic, of affection and certainty. The solid ground she clings to.

SEVENTEEN

The pity of it then that holidays must come with their sharp dislocation from all that is safe and comforting and orderly. Holidays, with the loneliness, the long hanging days. The anxiety to guess the requirements. To fulfil them. No lying around, no reading during the day, helpfulness please, helpfulness. Fresh air and exercise. No friends, no rehearsals, no bells and ranks and signals. Make yourself useful, Matti, make yourself useful.

'Matti, my dear. I have a little job for you today. Come upstairs to the study and I'll explain it to you.' Sinking heart. A little job. She knows them. It will be long and tedious. 'I'm preparing an article for the journal, Matti. It is to be illustrated with diagrams of the heart. I'm particularly interested in the superior vena cava and...'

'I'm not a very good drawer, Daddy.'

'My dear girl, you do biology at the convent. A little care and attention to detail is all that is necessary.'

'But...' But what? Why does she do it? Ssh, Matti, ssh.

'I am sorry, my dear, to find you stubborn. It is just this selfishness, Matti, that time and again I am forced to refer to. Can you not even do this for your old Dad who asks very little of you? Sit down. Sit down this minute. You will copy this diagram. It must be done in black ink. Use this special pen and nib. I shall return, Matti... What was that, my dear?'

'Nothing.'

'What did you say?'

'Nothing.' She sees his face. 'Oh, I said, like General MacArthur.'

'Be that as it may, I shall return to see how you are getting on.'

Matti arranges the paper. She dips the nib in the ink. She starts to copy the diagram. The ink runs down the nib and blots her first, careful line. She crumples up the paper and starts again, more carefully. Her jaw is thrust forward in concentration, her tongue between her teeth. Carefully, carefully, she copies the diagram. It is finished. It is not quite as fat a heart as the one she has been copying, but a nice heart all the same. She blots it. Carelessly. The superior vena cava bit smudges, slightly. She considers. It's all right. She screws the cap on the ink bottle and stands.

He enters suddenly, that look of either anticipatory pleasure or displeasure upon his face.

'You have finished, Matti! So soon! Let me see.' He pulls the paper towards him. 'Oh, no, no, no, no, no. What is this supposed to be?' She turns sullen.

'That.' She points to the book.

'I am asking you to do a simple little drawing. It has to be perfect. Is that clear? Sit down and don't get up until it's perfect.'

He leaves the room as briskly as he has entered it. She knows now. This is going to be a lot more difficult than she had hoped. She goes through the process again but on the final, careful downstroke the nib seems to spread itself into a harsh, scratchy line. She knows it must be discarded. She begins again. This time the superior vena cava is wiggly. Stupid thing. She tries again. So it goes. One bit right. Another bit wrong. He comes in again.

'Well? Finished?'

'It's hard. I can't do it. Can't I just trace it?'

'Certainly not. It's simply a matter of doing it properly, Matti. Slapdash will get you nowhere. It's a simple enough task. Do as I ask.' *Do it yourself.*

'Please, Daddy. I'm trying. I really am.'

And so she is, sitting in the sombre, dark room. Being rid forever of this rusty-smelling ink, this drawing paper, this textbook, this wayward nib, seems the most important thing in the world. Superior vena cava, posterior, anterior, interior, exterior, Lake Superior, inferior . . .

On and on and now she starts to grow tearful that the task will never be completed. Her hand trembles with anxiety, the line quavers. Another one ruined. In and out he goes, anger and resolution in his tread. With scarcely a glance he crumples up the papers that litter his desk.

'You will remain here until it is done to my satisfaction. It is a simple task. I will not tolerate your wilful ways. I will not tolerate them...'

Indeed he will not. Matti spends the day in the room. At lunch he brings her a glass of milk and a sandwich and tells her to apply herself. She applies herself. What seem to her perfect, absolutely mirror-image copies of the diagram in the book are ruthlessly discarded by him. Why? Is it beyond him to say, thank you, at last you've done a good one, thank you? Perfection is elusive, it seems. As her fear grows, the drawings deteriorate, her anxiety worsens. Now she is sobbing hopelessly, unable to draw at all.

'Let me stop. Please let me stop.'

'Stop the nonsense! You may stop when you have done as I ask. I ask very little, Matti. A little pleasantness, a little graciousness, in undertaking a task. You refuse to co-operate. You force me to be firm. You force me. I hate unpleasantness.'

The day wears on. She is not going to succeed now. Both of them are beyond success now. But she knows this before he does and gives up. Amid the welter of paper, the blots and smudges, the fat, thin, bulging, bursting, bleeding, broken vena cavas, she puts her head on the desk and waits for the storm to pass over.

For three days she is confined to her room and left alone, except to appear at meals. Which is small relief as he has told the family that Matti is in disgrace and not to be spoken to or acknowledged in any way whatsoever. Her little brothers stare at her with round eyes, made nervous by his edict.

The episode taints the rest of the holiday for her. She longs to return to her haven at school. *I did wrong. I did not draw it the way he wanted. I know that was wrong. I did not smile and embrace the task with gladness and graciousness. But was it so wrong that I am made to feel I do not exist in this place? That I am so unacceptable? I was wrong. I know it. I know it. But was I this wrong?* She torments herself with questions.

EIGHTEEN

It is only a few weeks into the new term when, one morning, as she pulls back the bedclothes to strip her bed, Matti sees, like a copper coin lying on her bed, a perfectly round stain. *It has happened.* She stands quite still, her heart thudding, excitement and a strange sinking feeling fighting it out inside her. Then practicality takes over. Imagine if anyone saw it! Quickly she rips the sheet from the bed and bundles it, stain hidden with the rest of the bedclothes, onto the chair outside her alcove. She will sponge it with her wet face cloth after her shower and if it is still wet tonight, she will lie on a towel. Gingerly she peers into her pyjama pants. A russet stain has spread along the seam. She feels messy and awkward. She wants to be mothered and organised. Yet, fleetingly, she gives thanks that this has not started at home. The very idea makes her skin crawl.

She fumbles in her cupboard for the brown packet. As her fingers touch it, it gives a tell-tale rustle. She freezes, listening. The silence around her is heavy with ears. Carefully she pulls a long, bulky pad from the packet and, holding her breath with anxiety, trusses herself up. She feels ugly and wounded and hopes no one will guess. She also feels proud. *I'm grown up. I belong.*

Later in the morning she makes her way to the linen room where eccentric Mother Martin presides over the shop where toilet articles can be purchased and recorded on account. Matti is embarrassed and the thing between her legs impedes her. On her way, two upper firsts saunter past and while one carries her packet casually under her arm, the other actually tosses hers in the air. Matti enters a linen room crowded with girls, all speaking at

113

once, all waving their arms, trying to catch Mother Martin's attention and be served.

'Who is next now? Who is next? And what might you... Put that brassiere down... and stop waving your arm... Who is pulling my veil? I will wait for silence. PUT THAT BRASSIERE DOWN... Now, where was I?' Mother Martin keeps up a monologue, admonishing, muttering, commenting, eyes darting, eyebrows permanently raised out of sight under her wimple. Matti stands towards the back. How can she possibly ask for what she wants in front of everyone? But the crush does not lessen and she is pushed nearer and nearer the front. Now she stands before Mother Martin.

'Who is next? Leave the linen room, that child there with... I BEG YOUR PARDON. Leave at once. What do you want? Speak up, child, speak up. PADS. How is your dear mother? What was it again? Oh yes, pads.' She turns to rummage through her supplies. Matti's cheeks burn. 'New-fangled American ideas. That's all I can say. New-fangled Am... WILL YOU BRING ME THAT BRASSIERE AT ONCE.' Carelessly she hands the packet to Matti and turns her attention elsewhere. Matti slides it under her pinafore, her ears hot with embarrassment. She hurries to the dormitory, torn, longing to toss it in the air, so proud she feels.

It is not long, however, before her embarrassment leaves her and she joins the camaraderie of those who have it. She can laugh and shudder with the others at the primitiveness of 'posting a letter' as she shoves the sodden, crushed mass of lint through the slot in the old wooden boxes that hide in the dark of the toilets. Like the others, she raises her eyebrows in disgust at 'Santa Claus', the half-blind, toothless old man who creeps through the school on Friday afternoons, emptying the letter-boxes into a vast hessian sack that he hoists across his shoulders, limping around the corridors and finally disappearing down the Tower Stairs, a hobgoblin creature with his loathsome cargo.

Matti learns how to make the episodes easier, less prone to accident. She learns how to wear two pads at once to lessen blood-stains. She learns how to smother pads in baby-powder so there is no tell-tale odour. She learns how to tuck extras into her suspender-belt so that she can change more frequently. She learns, although she never experiences them, how to feign cramps so that Sister in the infirmary gives permission for a siesta during recreation. It is a claustrophobic world of young women and Matti blooms in it.

Although not in that other world. She supposes she must tell her mother. 'Remember, Matti. Keep yourself clean. Clean. Don't leave anything lying around for the little boys to see. This is very private and you are not to discuss it. Collect your used pads and when it is over, light the incinerator and burn them.'

Matti dreads the bleeding at home. Rather than light the incinerator and acknowledge the thing that has happened to her, she stores them up. Bundles of blood, wrapped in toilet paper, mount at the back of her wardrobe, stale and foul. When no one is around, she smuggles them out of the house in her basket and dumps them in council bins. She learns from home there is disgust and distaste attendant on being a woman.

Matti flourishes in the predictability of the school year. But another of home's unpredictabilities now confronts her. Matti goes home for her regular Sunday visit. She senses the tension as soon as she arrives. The little boys are around but seem quieter than usual. Daddy is nowhere to be seen. What is it? As usual Matti joins her mother in the kitchen as soon as she arrives. There is the big Sunday dinner to prepare, roast chook, potatoes, pumpkin, tomato and onion pie, cauliflower and white sauce, thick, wonderful gravy. And of course pavlova to decorate with thick mounds of whipped cream and sliced banana and drizzles of passionfruit. Each Sunday it is the same, but today there is something different in the kitchen, something electric that flows through the whole house.

Matti looks sideways at her mother as they stand together over the stove, her mother stirring the white sauce, she the gravy. Pleasant smells envelop them, steam rises. Cosy. But, Mrs Milton leans forward and rests her forehead against the mantel over the stove. She raises her arm, spoon and all, and covers her eyes. She makes a sound. Could it be a sob? Matti is alarmed. She has never seen her mother cry. Tentatively she reaches out her hand and touches her mother's shoulder. Mrs Milton straightens her back and puts down her arm.

'What's wrong?'

'Oh, nothing, Matti. Nothing.' She shakes off the hand. But her eyes glisten with tears, although they do not fall, and a strangled, groaning sound comes from her throat.

'There is. There is. What is it? Oh.' An extraordinary thing happens. Mrs Milton drops the spoon and reaches out and drags her daughter to her. Tight she holds her. Tight. Matti is afraid and overwhelmed. Her mother has never held her like this. In her arms. Matti puts her arms around her mother's thin back and clings. And thus they remain for a minute or so. Then Mrs Milton lets go and pushes her hair behind her ear and takes up the spoon again. Matti waits.

'It's your father and me, Matti. We're not getting on at present. I'm worried. There's no one I can turn to for help.' *There's me. There's me.* 'I told him, a long time ago, that... that relations... you know... relations, babies...' she gestures helplessly, 'that all that was over and done with. One day you'll understand, Matti. So that was the end of that. But now he asks me, what's he supposed to do? Men! That's their trouble. Supposed to do! All they think about! No, I refused. I've finished with all that sort of thing. So, well, he's moved into the spare room. He's been in there all week. He won't speak to me. Never a word. Says he'll stay there. I don't...' She stirs the sauce with a frenzy. 'Well, this won't buy the child a dress.' Matti is speechless. *Her mother and father?* 'Get on with that gravy, Matti. It'll go all lumpy. Now, don't go mentioning this to anyone. The nuns at school or anyone. This is private. In the family. You mustn't mention it.'

Matti speaks, 'I won't.'

They sit to a silent family meal. Even her brothers are subdued and watchful. Matti is terrified. Another predictability might break apart.

She returns to school. Her mother drives her back. Her father has disappeared again.

'Remember, Matti. Don't mention this to anyone. It's just in the family. It's private.'

'I won't. I won't.'

The burdens seem heavier than ever. She prays, she cries in the privacy of the alcove, smothering the sound in her pillow. She thinks and worries and wishes she was at home, to watch, to note, to help, to hug and hold and feel the need. By Thursday she is unable to contain herself. She must ring and find out if they are happy again. But children are forbidden to use the phone except in the direst emergencies and only with permission. So be it. She makes an appointment with the Mistress of Discipline and lies shamelessly.

'My mother had an operation this week and...' Mother Anton raises her eyebrows in surprise. Normally parents inform the school of such things. 'And I am worried about her and want to ring and see that she is all right.' Mother Anton does not believe the girl but she gives her consent. Sometimes it is necessary.

After night prayers Matti collects the key to the phone room and makes her call.

'I've been so worried. I can't think...' And she starts to cry, big sobs of pain.

'Matti. Listen to me now. You haven't discussed this with anyone?'

'No.'

'Good girl. Listen, I'm going downstairs now to talk to Daddy. I'm going to tell him he must stop this. I'm going to tell him how upset you are. Everything is going to be all right. Are you listening? Everything will be all right now. Do you hear?'

'Yes.' In a whisper. 'Will I wait on and you can come back and tell me what he said? If it really is all right.'

'No, you hang up now. We'll see you as usual on Sunday and you'll see. Daddy has been very selfish to behave in this way but when I tell him how upset you are he'll have to change his ways. Goodnight now. No more tears. Off you go. Goodnight, Matti.'

'Goodnight.'

Matti hangs up and sniffs and blows her nose and hopes. And a little part of her swells with happiness that her mother could treat her like this, like an important partner, someone who is needed and leaned on.

NINETEEN

All the more reason after this unpredictability to cling to, look forward to, all the predictability that the school has to offer. It is Reverend Mother's Feast. It starts the evening before with a Wishing. The girls have prepared feast books and exhibitions in honour of the superior. They have sung to her and presented tableaux and given her flowers and filed silently to the dormitory with white veils draped over their arms to wear to a celebratory Mass in the morning.

Shortly after dawn, through each dormitory and along the passages, a raucous clanging breaks out. Girls are streaming through, parting alcove curtains, swinging clappers, blowing whistles, ringing bells. The shock of the clamour ejects sleepers from their beds and within seconds the whole school is racing, pulling on gowns, slipperless, to the main staircase. They pack themselves onto the cold stairs, laughing and shouting. The nuns stand about smiling, making no effort to silence them. Then some of the upper first step forward and present a series of skits on the nuns. The girls listen and laugh and part of the excitement is the tremor that runs through them all that the nuns can possibly allow this, will tolerate mimicry and jokes at their expense. But like any time out of season, the conditions have altered for just a little while.

After Mass they collect huge wicker baskets from the kitchen, containing the feast day breakfast. Hard-boiled eggs, crisp rolls that crackle as they are torn apart to reveal the snowy white, warm bread inside, fruit and pots of foaming milk coffee. All the nuns seem to be smiling and even the white-veiled novices who are usually on silent washing-up duty are laughing and talking among themselves as they collect the empty baskets. It is a feast day and the girls can wear coloured ribbons in their hair and ankle socks instead of lisle stockings. Heaven.

After breakfast they prepare for *cache-cache*. The entire school is divided into two huge teams and several young nuns are leaders of the teams. The nuns have folded back their sleeves and pinned up their skirts like panniers so that their white petticoats are revealed. They have anchored their veils more securely with huge hat pins and changed into sandshoes. Mother Anton assembles the teams in front of Queen's Square and reads out the rules of the game. Then the bell rings and the game starts.

Before lunch the game is halted and the girls race upstairs for midday showers.

'I've never seen anything so stupid,' sniffs Flynn, appearing from her alcove where she has been reading a contraband book all morning. 'It's so babyish. Imagine playing hidings.' Matti giggles uncertainly. Part of her agrees with Flynn. But she has enjoyed the game. The belonging. She admires Flynn for not needing to. She giggles again and shrugs. She doesn't want it spoilt.

She throws herself into the activities of the day. The talent quests, the literary quizzes, the treasure hunt. When at last darkness falls, they picnic by the light of kerosene lamps on the lawn. They are permitted to linger over the meal and stretch themselves flat on the grass and then they move inside. Now they change into their night wear and collect their rugs and gather down in the dark passage outside the piano cells. One by one the nuns they know so well in the classrooms come to entertain them, some with ghost stories, some with songs and poems and guitars, some with stories of the convent long ago. As they listen they are lulled by a sense of continuity, a sense of belonging to a family with its own habits and odd ways, its own history, its own language even. Finally they trudge up the flights to bed, quietly collecting the hot milk and biscuits that await them in the dormitories. Tomorrow it will be as if it never happened. Until next year.

Next year and the next and the next. They honour the Sacre Coeur de Jesu with the Procession of the Lanterns, octagonal cardboard lanterns, with cut-out patterns pasted with cellophane. Inside each burns a fat candle.

'Hold your lanterns upright, children. We do not want wax all over the floor. Keep your veils away from the flame.'

'It's a wonder the place has not been burned down before now,' mutters Flynn, bored, but singing the hymns in her high, sweet soprano.

They honour the Feast of Mater Admirabilis. They file into Mater's chapel and kneel before the huge picture of the pink-clad virgin. As always Matti glances quickly to the back of the chapel to see if the special case is open. It is. She peers closely. It holds a wax head of the crucified Christ covered in tears and blood which run from his rheumy, suffering eyes. Girls have been known to weep with piety and devotion and think they might become nuns when they have knelt beside this representation. But it is rarely open, and certainly Matti has not been so moved or touched by grace.

Lent comes in with the smearing of ashes on their foreheads on Ash Wednesday. The smearing signals the descent of gloom and how they hate it! No more lollies to be offered round the table after dinner. No more birthday cakes to break the monotony of the meals. The nuns seem stricter than ever and silence is even more rigorously enforced. Rumour has it that the community scourge themselves and wear penances that bite into their arms and backs.

They march as usual to their dining tables, gloomy because there will be no talking this Ash Wednesday. They must 'offer it up'. Their meal awaits them. A large dish of sardines sits at the server's place. They are all served a portion and they smear their plates and try to eat as little as possible. As soon as they can they turn to the sweets. Large, purple grapes. They share them out and eat the lot.

The bell rings. Mother Anton is in the centre of the dining room, her cold dark eyes flashing.

'Every child will stop what she is doing.' Instantly there is silence, and motion ceases. 'I find it hard to believe my eyes. Today we prepare to remember the suffering of Our Blessed Lord. You all bear on your foreheads the symbolic representation of this act of atonement. And yet you all cast judgement on the food set before you. You ignore the opportunity to suffer with Our Lord and instead, satisfy your own selfish needs. I shall ask the Sister to serve up the sardines again tonight and you will have the opportunity to make recompense. You may now proceed with the packing up.'

The clatter of plates resumes as the scraping and stacking proceeds. Philomena Morgan, upper first and Blue Ribbon of Excellence, walks to the birthday cupboard and removes her cake. Today is her birthday. A breathless hush and stillness falls upon the room. Philomena senses it and stops in confusion and slow realisation. Her face flushes and she stands rooted. A tornado of black veil descends upon her, snatches the cake and thrusts it back into the cupboard. 'Whatever can you be thinking of?' Philomena weeps. In dejection, they file out.

And dejected they remain. Visits to the chapel, normally regular enough, are even more frequent. No more sitting during the Offertory of the Mass. They compare the bumps on their knees. They pick at the flaky roughened skin that has formed. They bemoan the indignity of it all. Masses are solemn affairs, no singing and all the statues bagged in purple sacks. The only interest is in the umbrella Mother Anton carries outside the chapel to ward off a bat that has taken to diving onto the nuns' veils.

In this season they carry the New Testament and study it, muttering to themselves. They must learn and recite the Passion Gospel before Reverend Mother on Good Friday.

Lent limps into Holy Week. On Holy Thursday night they gather in the study room and Mother Anton addresses them all.

'Tonight you will make up for Our Lord's disciples who were unable to stay awake and watch with Our Lord as He went through the Agony in the Garden before His Passion and Death. "Could you not watch one hour with me?" He asked his disciples. How little He asked. But they were unable to give Him that. Tonight you will atone for that act of great selfishness.'

They are woken at midnight. They fumble, sleepily, for their clothes. The lights are dim and as they move through the dark passages they are imbued with solemnity and awe. Into the chapel they go, the sanctuary lamp a pin-prick of red in the distance. They kneel and from the wooden-carved choir stalls around the side, the lament of Tenebrae arises, flooding and fading, flooding and fading on the night, the centuries-old cry of desolation rising to the rafters and the Redeemer.

The air prickles with emotion. The kneeling girls strain to see the nuns who crouch in their stalls, their veils thrown over their faces like grieving widows. On and on the sound weaves until a tremendous battering sound breaks upon them. 'When the cock crows thou wilt deny me thrice,' and the nuns beat the wood of their stalls with their Books of Office, a beat of terror and desperation and despair.

The girls stumble, giddy with emotion and fatigue, from the chapel to their beds. Later, Mother Anton will do the rounds, shaking the more reactive among them from their self-imposed penance on the cold, hard floor, back under the covers of their warm, hard beds.

They spend Good Friday in silence and religious ritual and recitation of the Passion Gospel. Then they return to the chapel to remember the hour of His death.

It is done. Over. The hour of three o'clock, the hour of death is passed. They file from the chapel and out the doors of Queen's Square. 'Happy Easter. Happy Easter.' They grab their cases and stream to the waiting cars, to sunshine, noise, a gluttony of chocolate, a living, vibrant, carefree world, outside.

Matti feels the sun on her face. She hears the laughter and she goes through the motions of rejoicing. Then she stiffens herself for the confusion and the menace and the new unknown rules that must surely manifest themselves to her over the short Easter holiday.

TWENTY

In the family home the ageing woman lay sleepless. Anxiety, anger thrummed through the base of her skull and her shoulders. Exhaustion held her rigid with tension. How much longer could he last? She had supported him, nursed him, fed him, humoured him, as best she knew how. As she had done all her life. How much more would be asked of her? She felt that soon she must surely burst with resentment at the cheat her life had turned out to be. And underneath these thoughts, always, always, was the fury with her daughter. The daughter who had confused them, terrified them, defied them, then escaped, leaving her to pull the strands together again, support him, support him, always support him.

And now this daughter was back, breezing in as easy as you please when all the hard work was done, at no cost to herself, free as a bird. Mrs Milton's body was flooded with outrage. There she was in there with him now, whispering God knows what into his ear, and him helpless, having to listen. But he'd want to listen. Oh, yes he would. Hadn't she always been the favourite, the one he lived for? Hadn't she always been able to twist him around her little finger, getting her own way, wearing him down with her sulkiness and her obstinacy, blackmailing him with her outrageous behaviour? While she, the mother, who had none of these ploys, these tricks, had stood back and slaved, slaved. For what? To be second best! Oh, yes, her daughter, her wretched daughter, she was the one. Mrs Milton switched on the bedside light in agitation, afraid of how she felt towards her only daughter.

In the hospital the father drifted in and out of awareness. There was barely any time left now. He was tough. Life was tough. And he'd attacked it knowing that. And he had won. He was at peace. The fullness of time had come and soon he would die and he was ready and waiting.

Desmond could not sleep despite the warm, restful body beside him. He thought about his sister and how little he knew her. Really knew her. His mother had started to confide in him years ago when he was still in the seminary, writing him long letters of confusion and worry. Matti had done such and such and what were they going to do now? Matti was ungrateful and intransigent and hospitalised and oh, the shame, the disgrace, the worry, the worry, the worry. Desmond had read the letters and written soothing replies, drawn from his knowledge of the gospels and the great thinkers of the church. What more could he offer then? He had entered the seminary straight from school, and never held a girl's hand, in fact knew almost nothing at all about what the world could toss up for people to cope with. Desmond shuddered, but smiled too, at his total naivety. Well, he had done the best he could. He knew Matti second-hand, really. And all those letters had been so long ago. What was it? Twenty-five years ago.

He, Desmond, had developed a modus operandi. He led his life as a priest as best he could and if he had to have a secret life as well, to help him cope, well . . . But there were rules to it. It must be totally discreet. For a decade it had been thus. There was no reason to think that it could not remain so. And that was the same attitude he had towards his sister. I don't care what you do so long as you do nothing to upset this family, especially my mother, who has had enough. Do you hear? Enough! Who has been a model of rectitude and courage. He was grateful to her and as long as his sister did nothing to hurt or distress her, then he could accept Margaret's presence at this time. And he had told her that and just had to hope she would comply. If he had known her better, hadn't been away during the bad years, and then she hadn't been away once he finished in the seminary, then, who knows? They might have got to know each other better, recaptured some of the sharing that they had done as little children. Still, there you go. They had been apart and that had created a chasm too wide and too deep ever to be bridged. It was going to be a difficult few days. He sighed, reached out his hand and pulled the warm, soft body towards him.

Margaret stretched and walked quietly from the room, in search of a cup of coffee. She would not sleep tonight and she didn't want to but her mind teemed with the memories and she sought some relief. From the ones that were building and needed to be looked at once more. She baulked at the prospect. *It was then that I started to really fall apart. I started to disintegrate and only I knew it. And why? Was it so terrible? Would another person have fallen apart as I did?* But she knew the question was purely academic. She had and that was all there was to it. It was how she, for better for worse, had handled her life and perhaps now, she could put it all away forever and ever and ever.

TWENTY-ONE

Home for Easter. Doctor Milton will dine alone with his daughter. His wife is upstairs in bed, debilitated with vicious sciatic pain that overwhelms her with agony when she tries to move. Matti has put her younger brothers to bed and reassured her mother that they are covered up and sleeping. She has taken the bottle to her youngest brother and held him, still half-asleep, guiding his little willie into the wee bottle. She has sat on the end of Desmond's bed — he has the mumps — and tried to talk to him but he has a good new book to read. At her mother's request she has waited up for her father, kept late at the hospital, to prepare his evening meal and serve it to him.

Downstairs it is dark and quiet and warm. She sits in the glow of a dying fire and waits. Secure, lulled. And now he has come and she has grilled his steak and removed the vegetables from the oven where they have been waiting, covered by a saucepan lid to prevent them drying out. She worries slightly about what to give him for sweets. Dr Milton has forbidden the serving of tinned food for dinner as the sign of slovenly housekeeping. Quickly she beats up a custard and slides it into a pan of water in the oven to set. That and some cheese and biscuits will be acceptable.

Now her father has finished his tour of the upstairs regions and comes into the kitchen.

'You'll forgive me, Matti, if I take off my tie. I've had a long day.' She smiles at him and bustles. It is one of those precious times when she believes she might be able to do everything perfectly. She is excited and proud. She carries him a bottle of beer and a beaker on a silver tray as she has been taught. When he has finished she removes it and he moves to the dining room for his meal.

It is a dark-papered room lit by an old green and black glass lamp. Matti likes this room because of the secret on the wallpaper. She knows that on the dark paper, at intervals, are drawings of grasshoppers that blend, chameleon-like, into the trellis of vines that wind over the paper. She has tried many times to count the grasshoppers and always gets a different answer. One day she will get it right. Now she is sitting with her father, alone and loving him and waiting for his praise.

'That was very nicely done, my dear. You can do things properly when you set your mind to it.' *For a caress in your voice, I will do anything.* She sets the custard before him and the cheese and biscuits. He pushes back his chair.

'Wait here, my dear. I have something to show you.'

She is surprised. He runs lightly up the stairs and she hears his footsteps overhead in his study. She waits, crunching on a biscuit. She hears him switch off the lights upstairs. Everyone is sleeping.

He returns. Now it is only the two of them who exist in this house, held in a circle of light in a dark room. He has a book in his hand.

'I want to show you some pictures, Matti.' He flicks through the book until he finds a sequence of pictures. He places the book under the light. Matti looks at them, puzzled. 'This is what the Germans did to the Jews, Matti.' She stares mesmerised, her heart pounding with slow, measured thumps. *What is this? Why is he showing me this? Why?* 'Look here, Matti. You see how the women were treated.' She looks in horror. Naked women, in the act of running. Bald-headed. Obscene patches of black between their legs. Panic starts to rise in her. *Don't show me. Let me go back to the time before I saw this. Let there be light and noise and the rest of the family milling around.*

'The doctors were amongst the worst of them.' His voice is quiet and bland, silky almost. She stares at frightful pictures of limbs, hideously mutilated, all the more terrible for not seeming to be attached to a body. *What sort of face would look up at me from this page, that bore such butchery on its limbs?*

And he is not yet finished. He flicks over to another sequence of pictures. He shows her scenes of people lying on snow-covered ground.

'They found, Matti, by experimenting with prisoners, that the best way to warm a frozen person, prevent hypothermia—dying

127

from cold—was with the warmth of another body. They were trying to find a way to save airmen who were shot down over the North Sea. See here, a man with two women. They measured their responses and never cared that they died. They were actually experimenting on human beings.'

All the people in all the pictures are naked. Matti can scarcely believe that this scene is taking place. He who rules so ruthlessly on modesty for his daughter, shows her these. Over and over go the pages, each seemingly more appalling than the page before.

'Now Matti. I want you to promise me something. I have not shown you everything in this book. You are not old enough. And the text is very medical and specific. I want you to promise that you will never take this book off my shelf. Is that clear? You will never look at it?'

'Yes, Daddy, yes.'

'And another thing. I do not want you to tell your mother about what I have shown you. She would not understand my reasons. She would say it was unsuitable for a girl. But I believe you need to know about these things.' He rises and goes back up the stairs. She registers that he is taking care to be very quiet. She sees him crossing the study and carefully reinserting the book into its space on the bookshelves.

Shaken, she clears away the dinner things. A lesson? What is the lesson? The secrecy, the promise extracted, seem to increase the enormity of the horror. She feels defilement and shame—a terrible knowledge that he has burdened her with and no one with whom she can share it—except him. And if she shares it with him, what other horrors might he expose her to? She is wretched and further apart than ever and gripped in the silent house by an almost unbearable loneliness. And above all, she sees the running women, their sex a hideous black bull's-eye on the depersonalised bodies in the snow.

Returning to school after Easter, Matti feels a rebellion stirring in her that, for the first time, she does not ignore. She is angry and critical and full of hate. *But what do I hate? Who do I hate?* So she must look for victims. Disliking herself more and more as she stalks. She must choose the helpless so she can be powerful and ruthless and absolutely safe. And this short-sighted, uncoordinated girl who cannot read is her first victim. She sits at the same meal table as Matti, and Matti persecutes her, bombarding her with questions, in the politest voice, meal after meal. The same questions, over and over and over. At first the girl is flattered and then confused. She understands that for some reason she is being mocked and she is powerless before her polite interrogator. Week in, week out. But finally Matti is bored with such submissive prey.

The piano cells stretch in the gloom along the bowels of the building, close by Nazareth and Bethlehem. Each cell contains a piano and a chair and a metronome, with one small, heavily-barred window looking onto the bleak night. Down here is an underworld of hidden passions that never see the light of the real world upstairs in the study room.

Down here, in two shifts a night, twenty girls sit and play their scales, their arpeggios, their studies and preludes and fugues. Down here, too, the girls escape the eternal surveillance, for no one watches them but one of Reverend Mother's friends from 'outside', a disturbed, incapable young woman.

Here is place and space, time and opportunity for cruelty. How the girls ape and mock the young woman and her unwieldly walk, the stammering voice, the tensely clutching hands, the eyes that roll and widen like a nervous horse. Matti excels in the impersonations. She revels in the tormenting and the acclaim. Down here. In the dark. During the day she is another Matti who spares no time in thinking of the night and the evil. Compartments, divisions. They are what keep life orderly and manageable. So, every night she assaults the woman anew and the woman seems to invite it, await it, frozen, petrified like a mouse before a snake. Matti the powerful. The ruler. The judge. The executioner. The woman will say nothing. She needs all her strength just to keep on coping. Night after night Matti is caught up in the excitement of this dark undertow, the relish of her chance for hurtful, hateful power. It is furtive and cowardly and a source of disgusted joy and exhilaration.

Tonight Flynn and Matti are in their cells, Matti fumbling over the trills and Flynn playing her Bach with fluency and grace and quiet gravity. Mother Sweeney, with her huge ring of keys, has clanked by on her nightly rounds, securing the many doors and windows of the convent. Matti and Flynn, now bored with the piano practice, stand together in the dark passage, seeking distraction. Quietly they open the cupboard where the tennis racquets are stored. They extract two from their presses, take a ball, and pat it back and forward between them. The novelty palls. But they have attracted attention, as they had hoped to do. From the far end of the passage they hear the clump, clump of feet. They climb into the cupboard and wiggle themselves into the mesh of a tennis net that lies there. It is suffocatingly dark and there is a smell of tar. In unison, they start to moan. The footsteps hasten, pause, hasten again and they hear doors being opened. They moan louder, then wait, then moan again. Their victim throws open the door and sees a tennis net twisting and heaving. 'Come out. Who's in there? Come out.' They can hear her panting and gasping and it excites them. 'Come out at once.' Surely they can feel her hot breath as she peers into the blackness. They rock and moan. Suddenly they hear her move away and know she is fumbling for a light cord. Swiftly they untangle themselves and move at a stumbling, crouching run down the length of the cupboard. With what sounds like a neigh of triumph she abandons the search for a light and clumps down the outside of the cupboard, opening each door as she passes.

They stay one door ahead of her. Now they are near the Tower Stairs and will have to break cover to reach them. In total darkness they leap out and dash ahead of her for the wooden stairs. Up, up, up they pound, then stop and wait. Silence. Has she given up so soon? They sit and remove their shoes. It is as well to be as quiet as possible on the noisy wood. Tensely they wait, afraid that it might be all over. But, no. They hear the unmistakable clumping. She has doubled back, gone up the main stairs and is coming from above. They smile at each other, give a moan of triumph so that she knows she is on the track of her prey and creep noiselessly back down the stairs to the base where the Black Hole with its huge hessian sacks of cast-off paper and cardboard looms.

Trying to stifle their giggles, they cross the Black Hole and let down the side of the huge sack that hangs there. Into it they clamber, hearts beating, for they hear her now and she, too, has removed her shoes. It is the wheezy breath that gives her away. Nearer and nearer she draws and they crouch, holding tight to each other, scarcely breathing. For an age, it seems, she stands motionless, unable, uncertain, afraid, and Flynn and Matti find the tension almost unbearable. They can feel each other's heart pounding, their hot breath on each other's cheek. They are racing with excitement and thrill. Holding each other. As time and darkness hang waiting, breathless, silent, they find each other's lips and kiss, long and hard.

Then, shockingly, the silence is broken. Shoes back on. Clump, clump. They pull apart instantly. They wait. Silence again. Their hearts still pound. Their faces are flushed and they tremble. As quietly as possible they climb from the sack and creep towards the stairs.

'Ah!' It sounds like a cry of pain. 'I've got you.' She has been lurking. She pounces, grabs in vain but they are fleeter, healthier. Up, up, up the Tower Stairs they go. Up and up. They pause.

'Keep going, Matti. Quick!'

'We can't. It's Community up there.'

'She'll get us if we stop. Quick. Keep going! She'll never follow up here.'

So, up the final flight they go, terrified at their own daring. They reach the top and burst through the door into the nuns' private domain.

'Pooh!' says Flynn, bending over to catch her breath. 'Not much up here, is there?' Matti covers her mouth to suppress a giggle of nervousness.

'Only an old wheelchair. Let's have a go in it.'

'No, Flynn. No,' says Matti, firmly back in the real world. 'I think we'd better sneak back.' They put on their shoes and smooth their hair and down they go. They peer from the stairs into the main corridor. It is change-over time for the cells. Casually they join the ranks and enter the study room.

Down below, the woman gasps for breath and steadies herself by rocking back and forward on her heels. She clenches her fists and throws her head back wildly, gathering her strength for the next confrontation.

A term of it, a hateful, hellish, cold black term of it like an arctic winter. The following term the woman does not return and they are asked to write short notes to her wishing her a speedy recovery. Now there is no prey to stalk, no distraction from the hatefulness inside. The voices whisper to Matti. You are bad, Matti, so bad. Now you see, don't you, just how bad? Everything he says is true. You are wicked and cunning and . . . *No, I'm not. I don't want to be. I'm good and special. Aren't I? Like they have said so often. That's the person I like. The person I want to be. Am. Like they say.* They! Who are they? They haven't seen you like I have. From deep inside. I know. You know. We both know, don't we? Together we whisper secrets to each other. We know . . . *But don't tell! Please don't tell!* Not yet I won't. *Please no. Never. Leave me alone. Go away from me, from my heart.* How can I do that? I am you. I cannot leave you. Go. *Go away from my heart, my head. I hate you. I hate you. I hate you.* Ha! You make me laugh. How can I go? I am you. You hate me? You hate yourself. Matti. Hate yourself. Hate yourself.

TWENTY-TWO

The Milton family is having the usual Sunday baked dinner. Dr Milton decides to have some fun.

'Well, Mummy dear. What do you think Matti is going to do when she leaves school?' Matti's buttocks tighten on the dining-room chair. She would prefer these days that no attention were drawn to her. Nevertheless, she has to say it.

'I'm going to be an actress.' Her father ignores her.

'Well, Mummy? What do you think? A nice little lady doctor?'

'Don't be putting ideas into her head, Patrick.'

'What do you think, Matti? A nice little lady doctor, eh?' He laughs at the ridiculousness of it all.

'I'm going to be an actress.'

'Now, now. None of that. Let's see. What about a journalist, Mummy? Think Matti would make a good journalist?'

'For heaven's sake, Patrick. Matti is not to be a journalist. Terrible women. Tough. Not an ounce of femininity.'

Matti looks across at Desmond. He is eating his dinner and seems quite content. No need to worry about what Desmond is going to do. They all know that he is going to be a priest. Matti is tense and angry. *Yoo hoo. I'm here. Did you hear what I said? Did you hear what I said I wanted to be? Doesn't what I want matter at all? Maybe they did not hear. Maybe I am not really here at all.* She looks around the table, at her parents, her brothers. *If I stretch out my hand and try to touch you, will it reach? Will you feel my touch? Do you hear, do you understand the words that come from my mouth? Maybe I speak a language that you do not understand? Maybe I am not even here at all!*

'Well, Matti, and what do you say to that?'

'What?'

'Matti. Matti. Let's not start on the wrong foot.' He frowns. Mummy looks angrily at her. They say grace and leave the table. Matti and Desmond clear the dishes.

'Why don't you ever listen, Matti? No wonder they say you're sulky. It was about skiing. He's taking us skiing!'

'Skiing! How come? Why?'

'I don't know. But he is.'

At the start of the following holidays Dr Milton sets off to drive them both to the snowfields. An offer of accommodation has been made. He has accepted the offer—after much thought. He dislikes flamboyance. He thinks skiing may be flamboyant. However, on the plus side, mastering a new sport is a rigorous, disciplined exercise. It will do him good. It will do Matti and Desmond good.

His hands tighten on the wheel. Displeasure nudges at him. What will do Matti good? Heaven knows, he has tried. The girl is clumsy and sullen. No more fun at the dining table, entertaining them all, being a good sport and laughing at herself in a healthy manner. Not so much as a smile these days. The car slides slightly on the ice and he brakes too sharply. It slides out of control and comes to rest on a snowbank. The spinning wheels churn up muddy, crusty snow as he manoeuvres it back on the road. He is irritably conscious of Matti sitting in her usual place in the back. Take Desmond now. Dr Milton relaxes in pleasure. Despite those unpromising beginnings, he is developing into a fine lad, studious, polite to all and sundry and showing self-discipline beyond his years. Dr Milton has high hopes for him. He loves him for causing so little trouble. And his table manners, on home Sundays, are a credit to the good Fathers who educate him. Dr Milton muses on this as he drives along. His head nods, his lips move. He is well pleased here.

Matti sits quietly in the back. This event is such a novelty that she cannot help being excited. Perhaps she will even meet some boys! 'Boyos more likely,' Desmond has said, referring to his classmates who come to the snowfields in winter and apparently spend a great deal of the school term smoking behind the handball courts and necking with girls down near the rowing sheds. Desmond does not approve of them. You can tell that from his tone of voice. Nevertheless, Matti is dying to meet a boy. She sits in the back, dreaming.

'Matti. Hop to, dear.' They have arrived. Her father and Desmond are lugging the ski gear from the car. Her job is the foodstuffs. She will be in charge of the domestic side of things this holiday. 'I have booked a class for this afternoon. You only have half an hour to get the job done. Hop to.' Dr Milton strides restlessly up and down the kitchen while she stows the provisions. He makes her nervous and edgy when he does this. She wishes he wouldn't. But he always does it, even with her mother, at home. It makes her mother nervous too.

The Miltons do not have this ski lodge to themselves. The kitchen is communal and there are segregated bunk rooms. Matti shares hers with strangers, a girl who sits on her top bunk and eats food from a saucepan each night, and two gloriously lovely models who have the bottom bunks. Matti is terrified of them, with their poise and nonchalance. She pretends to be asleep when they come in at night and in the morning she is up and gone, to cook breakfast for Daddy and Desmond, long before they wake up.

But she is not asleep. Oh, no. She listens, she envies, she admires. The frothy lace of skimpy bras and wispy, hardly-there-at-all underpants, the long straight hair, the false eyelashes, the pale, pale lipstick against the snow-tanned skin. Matti covets their fur hats and luminous pink ski pants and wrap-around goggles. She is ashamed of her hired black pants and parka and her knitted beanie. She is ashamed of her whole self.

She lies in bed, eyes closed, afraid lest they flutter under the harsh light. It is too late now to admit that she is awake. The model girls have men in their bunks! There are giggles and groans and intakes of breath. Matti's body is hot and immobilised with embarrassment and the fear of what Daddy might say or do should he find out.

The noises stop. People move above the tiny room, dressing. The saucepan girl enters and climbs unceremoniously up onto her bunk.

'Who's she?' asks a model girl. Matti knows they mean her. She lies still.

'Oh, just some little prude,' sniffs the saucepan girl. Matti can scarcely breathe. Her eyelids flutter compulsively. She hates this little prude.

They have been here a week. Long days of bone-wearying, exhilarating exercise and early nights. Tonight some of the boyos have come to visit and are at this very minute playing music in the lounge. Matti longs for lipstick and false eyelashes and nonchalance. She sits on the periphery of the group, hoping she might be noticed, might . . . oh, anything.

'Matti, come here please.' She looks up. Her father beckons her from the kitchen door. 'Just what do you think you're doing?'

'Oh. Oh, it's all right Daddy. Desmond is there. They are friends of his. From school. They've come . . .'

'Be that as it may, what may I ask are you doing? We are hungry. We are waiting for our dinner.' Matti flushes. It is true. The dinner has gone completely out of her head. Still, it's not that bad.

'Can't I stay out here a while and . . .'

'At once.' She turns from him. *Put it on yourself if you're that hungry. You're not helpless.* She enters the kitchen. She peels the potatoes and puts them on to boil. Her mind is inside with the music and the murmur of voices. She puts the casserole in the oven to heat and lights the water under the peas. She pokes the potatoes half-heartedly. Ages. She slips back to the lounge. They have started to dance. Someone grabs her arm and she jiggles about. Dancing! Twirls, wiggles, underarms, spins. Someone turns the music louder. Desmond moves away from the noise with a book. Matti puffs with exertion and . . .

'Get out there at once!' A figure stands before her and actually pulls her out of the circle. 'At once!' She cannot ever, ever remember seeing such fury in his eyes. The snowfields become icefields, long slippery-sharp slides and she is racing down them, out of control. She narrows her eyes against their glare, blocks her ears at the tearing, rasping sounds. *Please stop me. Let me come back.* 'Take a look at the damage you have caused.' She forces her eyes to open in the harsh, blinding glare. He is holding a pea-encrusted, blackened saucepan beneath her face. Matti recoils. She sees that he is actually shaking with rage.

'I'll clean it,' she says, in panic. 'I'll clean it.'

'How dare you! How dare you!' He is pacing like a caged tiger, up and down, up and down, the saucepan clenched in his fist. '"I'll clean it," you say, as if that will make up. I have been waiting, Matti. I have already had to remind you of your job. Now, through your lazy, selfish ways, we are presented with this disgusting mess. I . . .'

'I'll cook some more.' She is terrified.

'Do that, and be quick about it. This is the last holiday I will take you on. Your selfish ways are to cease this instant. Cook and cook quickly and woe betide you if I have to say another word.'

She cooks. She cringes from him. She longs to be gone from the terrible place of humiliation and evil. She longs to hide. Ice is about her, inside and out. There is no haven. And when at last they return home the disgrace must return with them for Dr Milton has to explain, more in sorrow than in anger, he says, that the holiday has been spoilt and Matti is to remain confined to the house and not be spoken to until school returns. The rest of the family obey him, angry with Matti for causing this tension in the family.

Thank God for the new term.

'How was it, Matti? How was the skiing? Did you meet any boys?'

'Oh. We didn't go, after all. Daddy had too many urgents. So we didn't go.' She is learning to dissemble and the more she does, the less she can control the terror.

The St Joseph's dormitory is inhabited by the older girls. It is not a floral dormitory like that one up there under the eaves. It is white and glary and the girls do not like it. But they love the bathroom that comes with it, a vast, marble-floored room with eight-foot-long, sunken baths, the aberration perhaps of some lonely Italian craftsman, building his memorial, far from home. The girls find it indulgent and cheering. It is the consolation prize for their cheerless dormitory.

At dawn one spring morning the dormitory wakes to the sound

of ill-concealed groans. Young Mother Clifton, whose thankless task it is to sleep in the end cubicle and maintain discipline, hears the sounds as she robes for the day. Deftly, she spears her veil to her bonnet, tugs the scratchy frill forward under her chin and hastens, beads clanking, towards the sounds. She pulls the curtains back and looks down at Helena Morrissey.

'What is it, dear?'

'I've got a terrible pain, Mother.' Mother Clifton hopes for reassurance.

'Do you get it every month, dear?'

'No.'

Mother Clifton looks at the glittering eyes, the flushed face. She sees the girl tense for another spasm.

'Stay where you are, Helena. I shall go down to the infirmary and get Sister.' She fishes in her skirts and finds her signal. Clack, clack, clack.

'Children, please rise quietly and prepare for Mass. I have to go to the infirmary. You are on your honour and I expect anyone who speaks to report herself to me when I return.' She hurries away.

They rise, listening to the uncomfortable sounds. They move uneasily, none daring approach the closed curtains. That she could make such sounds alarms them all.

Presently Mother Clifton returns, followed by the tall, starched, vulpine-faced Matron who runs the infirmary with cold, ill-concealed dislike for her patients. She is yet another of Reverend Mother's mendicants from 'outside' and illness among the girls is seen as a wilful attempt to interrupt her pleasant, book-reading life.

The girls hear her gruff voice in the alcove. She emerges and pulls the curtains back roughly. They see Helena Morrissey crawl out of bed, don her dressing gown and slippers and, as Matron watches, Helena rolls up her bedding. Matron nods curtly and strides out with her thermometer and her dignity, followed by a staggering bundle of bedclothes carried jointly by Mother Clifton and Helena.

That night, Mother Anton appears on the rostrum at the head of the study room. 'Put away your books, children. Reverend Mother is coming to see you.'

There is a buzz of surprise. Reverend Mother, so remote and grave, rarely seen outside Weekly Notes or chapel. 'In silence.' Clack, clack, clack. 'Stand behind your chairs.'

They wait and Reverend Mother enters.

'I have some very sad news, children. Our beloved child, Helena Morrissey, died in hospital this evening. Of peritonitis. Her very dear parents are waiting for me now in the parlour. I ask that you all make your way to the chapel and pray for the repose of her soul.' Reverend Mother bows gravely and departs. The girls stand in shocked silence, exchanging glances, wide-eyed. Dead? How can one of them be dead? The word thunders about them. Shock overflows into tears, tears that flow down faces unused to such sorrow.

Mother Anton stands before them again, white-faced and tremulous. 'Go along now, children. Go and talk to Our Blessed Lord.'

Speechlessly they flee.

The sanctuary is dark, the white marble of the altar glowing ghost-like. Around the sanctuary the statues hover and loom. Here and there nuns are dotted in the darkness, folded in stillness and silence and the black of their habits. How long the girls kneel there Matti cannot tell, but her own knees ache and her back is stiff and the tears have long since dried on her cheeks. She longs to sit down but cannot appear callous. Others still weep and sniff. A gentle clack, clack, clack.

'Let us pray aloud, children. We will recite the Litany for the Dead.' Reverend Mother leads the prayers and brokenly they respond. When it is over they file out and go to bed.

In the sterile St Joseph's dormitory they avoid looking at the empty space with open curtains. Matti watches the others. How do they feel? Do they feel? Really? (What would they say if she said that... that, almost, she didn't feel? Couldn't feel? That she too was dead? Would they say that something was very wrong with her?) But this whole process fills her with disbelief. Where is this girl now who has gone? Like some conjuring trick. Now you see it. Now you don't. But this is no conjuring trick. One minute you're alive and then, pouff, you're dead. Gone. Finito. And nothing changes. Everything just carries on. Day and night. Breathing in and breathing out. The world keeps turning, ignoring, careless of death. The very simplicity of it all is the most terrible part.

When Matti wakes next morning, her heart leaps. The sun is streaming through the windows, casting dappled patterns on the worn old floorboards. Birds are chirruping. The whole world is alive and loving it. Matti scrambles from her bed. She strips it and hauls the bedclothes to the chair outside. One look at Mother Clifton's face tells her she is mistaken.

'Oh, Margaret-Anne. Not so fast this morning, dear. Go back into your alcove and wait. There is to be a special Mass a little later this morning.'

Ashamed, she creeps back. God and the grave. God and the grave. Prayers and prayers and prayers.

But Matti does not want to pray. She wants to be in the classroom, reading *Jane Eyre*, discussing the Louisiana Purchase, dwelling on the lifestyle of the African Bushman, peering into the entrails of a rat, seeing how it all goes on and on and on.

Later, as they are dressing, Mother Anton enters the dormitory and cleans out Helena's cupboard. Inside her own alcove Matti pictures the process. Toothbrush, face washer, soap dish, pyjamas, underwear, perhaps with Helena's mark, her smell even, upon them still. Gone but not quite gone. Like hair and fingernails growing on a corpse. Disgusting thoughts. Solitary thoughts.

Mass is longer and more tedious than ever. Father Paul, the refugee priest, clad in black vestments, creeps through the Mass for the Dead and stomachs rumble in hunger. But when they finally eat their bread and jam and swallow their tea they are subdued. Reverend Mother makes another appearance. They rise and curtsey to her.

'Children, our dear Helena is coming home to us. His Eminence the Cardinal has permitted us to have the funeral in our chapel and Helena will be buried in the Community graveyard. The coffin will be in the chapel when you go upstairs. There will be no classes today but you are at liberty to come and go to the chapel as you wish.'

As you wish. Veils are produced from pockets and girls leave directly for the chapel. Matti wants class, ordinariness, certainty. She feels outside the pain and suffering, watching it as if in a play.

And her reaction confuses and frightens her. She goes to the study room to collect her veil and on her way she sees visitors approaching. As custom dictates, she moves to the wall and curtseys. A woman stops and speaks. Speaks so kindly.

'Thank you, my dear, for all your prayers. They are a great support to us. Helena loved you all.' Matti nods, unable to reply. This must be Helena's mother. She wants to tell her to go away, that she cannot pray because no prayers will come, that she was not Helena's friend. The woman pats her arm and moves away.

In the chapel the coffin is surrounded by candles. Matti kneels and presses her eyes with her finger tips. Through them she can watch the other kneeling figures. She can see the coffin. What does she look like inside there? How long before she turns horrid and blows up or smells or ... or what? Frightful. She herself is perverted. Obscene. *Pray, quickly, pray. Don't think these awful things. What is wrong with you?* And what about Helena, whom I thought was a princess? Helen of Morrissey I thought her royal name was, until one day I saw her name spelt out. What of her? Did she really love us *all*? Why didn't I love her back then? Why don't I love her now? Like everyone else does. Don't they remember her silly giggly laugh and the way she picked at scabs on her face, and how she shoved in ranks and jigged her foot so the desk shook if you were sharing with her? Now they are all crying and loving her and she is a saint and I am wicked, wicked, wicked to want her to go away.

Matti squeezes her eyes tight and prays for tears to come.

TWENTY-THREE

As Matti's final year approaches it is as if everything is unravelling despite her vigilance and determination. She hardly dares let down her guard for a moment. What has happened? The confusion and the questions from home have taken over her world even here in her beloved, predictable convent. Panic. Inexplicable, uncontrollable panic wells up in her daily. Terror of things she cannot name. Confusion that must be exploded if she is to go on. Exploded, momentarily, terribly.

Matti straggles at the end of the ranks for the dormitory. The worst time of the day. The time she will be alone with herself, with no routine or distractions from the questions that stab at her. Many of her classmates are peeling off to their rooms. Their rooms — as befits their status as senior girls. Why has she not been assigned a room? She had thought it was because some senior girls had to be in dormitories to set a good example. A pity. She would have loved to see her name on the Queen's Square board at the start of term assigning her to a room. Where she would be permitted to talk until lights out. Now she knows that she is not there to set an example. It is because . . .

'You Australian girls. You are so innocent,' the pasty, busty French girl with the sniff and the bitten nails had drawled scornfully the other day. 'You do not even know about lesbians.' Drawled it with scorn and disdain over the carpels and stamens in the lab. Sneakily, Matti had checked the Oxford English Dictionary in the library. Her heart had lurched! Nausea and terror! She and Flynn! In the Black Hole! So this is why she had no

142

room. They had guessed. They knew! But why then did Flynn have a room this term? *Help me. Help me. I can't keep . . .*

Clack, clack, clack goes the signal of the mistress on surveillance in the dormitory. The girls file into their alcoves for the night. Matti lays her veil, her missal and her gloves on her cupboard. The tension pounds through her. *Go away thoughts, please go away. Let me forget you for a minute. Give me some peace. Let me be a proper person. Leave me alone. Please. It is too much to bear.* She is screaming in terror inside her head. She must escape from the thoughts. Quickly she pulls on her pyjamas. Her stomach lurches with nausea. *Who am I? What am I?* All the sounds are screaming in her ears as she passes through the tunnel of ice. The ice is creaking, groaning, breaking apart around her. *Freeze up. Be still. Ssh. Ssh. Let met get my balance. Allow me, even for a second, freedom from my horrors.*

She waits in a fever of impatience until lights out. 'Good night and God bless you, Mother.' Furtively, she pulls open the drawer of her cupboard. Silently, well-practised, she withdraws her sewing kit. In the darkness she feels for the pins. Her fingers brush the blunt darning needle. She presses the pad of her finger on the sharp points of the scissors. No. Not that! Then she catches it on the pins. She withdraws one. She lays the kit on her cupboard and settles back on her pillow. Carefully, alert and tense, she rolls up her sleeve, up, up, into her armpit. Now, dreamily, slowly, deliberately, she positions the pin-point against the soft inner arm flesh. She takes her bottom lip between her teeth and rakes the pin harshly across her skin. The burn of pain assails her and she pulls away. Angrily now, she bites her lip harder and rakes again. Through the hot sear she feels a warmth on her arm. With her finger she touches the flesh. Heavy, viscous, sticky. For a moment her heart stops its terrible painful thumping. For a moment her stomach stops its nauseating churning. For a moment triumph overwhelms her. She grasps the moment. Viciously, hatefully, thrillingly, she tears her skin. Strip. Strip. Strip.

Peace and satiation envelop her. Almost in ecstasy she drops the pin to the floor. Mesmerised she winds down her sleeve. She has vanquished the demon. For the present. She slips deep under the bedcovers and falls asleep.

At home in the marital bed, Dr and Mrs Milton lie silent. Dr Milton loves his careworn wife. He longs to touch her. He has had a long day. A fraught day. Beside him Mrs Milton is untouchable. She has had a long day. A fraught day. A long tear of pain and confusion divides them.

Margaret rubbed her eyes wearily. Surely the first light of dawn would soon come into the sky. The huge plane tree outside the window had started to stir with the little breeze of early morning. She walked softly to the bed, not wanting to wake her father. Not until she had finished what she needed to do. She stood still and looked down at him. Then she turned away. It seemed almost indecent to be spying on him when he was so vulnerable.

She walked back to her chair and sat down again, sitting forward, staring out into the lightening sky. By the time that final school year came, I was sick. Sick. But there was no one I could explain my sickness to. It drew me into a dimension I did not even know existed. I was alone and terrified. I was going mad. Quietly, in a world of my own, I was going mad. And when they knew, it was too late to stop it. She glanced over at the bed. When he knew, even he, the all-powerful, was powerless. He couldn't do a thing. He didn't know how to. It was totally beyond his ken.

Her head was thrumming with memories. I hated you after, Daddy. I hated you through that year in the hospital when they fed me and cleaned me and clothed me. I hated you when you came and stood silently in that bare room where I crouched on a mattress. I did not permit myself to hear your words.

I hated you when I had to pick up the pieces of my life that lay scattered before me like a shattered tower of matchsticks. I hated you twenty-five years ago when you gave me the airfare and I went away. I hated you when I found that the only reason I had for living was to feed off my hatred towards you. I hated you for all the things you were not. And even when Robert came along, and the children, I found I was unable to let go the habit of that hatred. It kept me closed away and bitter so that you still controlled my life. I hated you that I allowed you that control. It was for me that I forgave, Daddy, for me.

As you lie there, coming to the end of your final test, I too come near to the end of a test. I want to say goodbye in peace and love.

TWENTY-FOUR

Mother Anton flexes her tense shoulders. She removes her steel-rimmed glasses and carefully polishes them on her large white handkerchief. Wearily she massages her eyelids with long, bony fingers. She replaces her glasses and looks at her list. A school year is starting and Mother Anton is thinking about her new upper first. They are her special province and the aspect of her life that gives her most pleasure. Her dual role, as Mistress of Discipline, she does not enjoy so much. The younger girls are a trial — noisy, giggly, flippant. Mother Anton is only really comfortable with order. The dimensions of her room, the placement of her papers, the severity of the furnishing, indicate this. Mother Anton is comfortable with right angles, straight lines, austerity. Young girls are not austere. The upper first, however, are ready for a hard year of study. They are more mature. She positively enjoys her time with them.

She aligns her ruler and puts a firm line through one of the names. Flynn O'Brien. She sighs. It is always a disappointment to lose one of them. Flynn, however, cannot stay at the school. She sits for a while thinking about the girl. From the word go the girl had been troublesome. Hadn't Mother Porter predicted trouble years ago? Mother Anton wonders if she dislikes the girl. No. It is not her place to like or dislike. Be that as it may, Flynn has been a constant nuisance. She has contributed little to the school spirit. Been untidy, unsettling, worked only sporadically. Flynn simply did not care about what the Sacre Coeur was offering her. If it did not sound over-dramatic Mother Anton would call her spirit anarchistic. Well, it's out of our hands now. She taps her fingernail on the desk in annoyance. Dear heaven she feels angry at the opportunities the girl has thrown away. She can write gripping and imaginative prose, she can sing, she can paint, her brain is alert and passionate and to what end? Writing rubbish in forbidden letters, singing at the top of her voice all over the school, defacing textbooks with ridiculous and childish drawings, taking on St Thomas Aquinas and Augustine in Christian Doctrine class, quoting a bit of this and a bit of that, half-baked theology and philosophy and scientology and goodness knows what else. Mother Anton likes her girls to question. You are at liberty to believe in the theory of evolution if you wish, she tells them at the beginning of the year. But, Flynn! A great, whirling mass of talents bubbling uncontrollably. No discipline. No order. One of the failures? Well, it is out of her hands now.

What an uncomfortable interview it had been with those poor parents. Bewildered and shocked by their daughter's behaviour. Imagine! Finding her in the marital bed with a long-haired student from the nearby campus and beer and cigarettes all over the carpet! Dear dear dear dear dear.

The poor souls asking her to talk to Flynn, make her see sense, and the girl coming, bold as can be, with her eyebrows shaved off and her hair dyed blonde and false eyelashes and black all over her eyelids and white lipstick and close-fitting clothes with black stockings and, oh dear God, a gold chain around her ankle! There was little Mother Anton could do. She knew that before she spoke to the girl. So Flynn was off to the country to the Dominicans for her final year. Wonderful nuns with a reputation for handling difficult girls. Mother Anton massages the bridge of her nose. It is always sad when something like this happens. Sadder still for the parents who had such high hopes. Still, with God, nothing is impossible. Mother Anton will remember Flynn in her prayers.

Which brings her to a consideration of the next name on her list. Margaret-Anne Milton. She marks a room number beside the name. Margaret-Anne has been an excellent example to the younger ones in the dormitory and as a reward for having to wait so long for a room, she gives her the tower room. All reports indicate that she will be taking on an intelligent and consistent student here. A child who was known to be a bit of a flibbertigibbet back in Junior School but who has settled down quietly now, giving no trouble at all. Mmm. No trouble at all? Mother Anton has found, from experience, still waters run deep in those who are no trouble at all. She will keep an eye on Margaret-Anne.

Margaret-Anne is also one of the girls who has been awarded the coveted Blue Ribbon for continued good behaviour and excellence in studies. Mother Anton has personally rung all the parents of such girls and told them the good news prior to the term starting. She sits back to consider. She wonders how Margaret-Anne is taking the news. Mother Anton has not been out of the convent gates since she entered thirty-one years ago. She has never entered the home of a pupil. She has never taken a meal with anyone but the Community in all that time. She cannot imagine what a family meal is like today.

The Miltons are sitting around the dinning table and Dr Milton has something to say.

'Well, Matti. Your mother and I are mighty pleased that you have been awarded a Blue Ribbon. It means that the nuns are aware that you show promise. It's a great privilege, my dear. Now's your chance to show what you're made of. The Mothers know you well, Matti.'

The girl tightens inside herself. *How well do they know me?*

'They are as aware as I am of your selfish little ways. That, unfortunately, I've had to refer to from time to time. This could be the making of you. Give this year all you've got. Grit your teeth and get on with it and bring credit on us all. As Desmond has done.'

That's right, babble away. I'm not listening. Why should I? I know it by heart. I hear you loud and clear, but I'm not listening. She looks at him, his mouth opening and closing, words issuing forth into the emptiness.

Emptier still, since Desmond has gone. Oh, what a Christmas it has been. The pangs of departure hanging over them all. She misses him and she did not know she would. But Desmond has been a solidity in her world. Through his diligence and dignity he has made her father proud and that has recompensed for her. He has deflected the father from the daughter by his excellence and she is grateful for that. He has promised that he will ask permission to write letters to her and that he will pray for her and be her friend always.

'Come on, my dear. A little graciousness is all I ever ask. Once upon a time, Matti, you used to give us such pleasure at the meal table. Didn't she, boys?' He looks cheerfully around at his sons, insignificant dots on Matti's horizon. They nod. They don't care much.

'Remember, dear. All work and no play makes Jack...'

Shut up and close your mouth while you're eating. I'm sick to death of your happy little sayings, your quiet, reasonable all-for-your-own-good voice. Oh, yes, I know. The most reasonable of men. Well, you can be, can't you? You've got it all your own way. Well, you bully, you don't know it, but old front-row forward, good ol' sailor, hasn't forgotten. Whatever I did, you wanted something else. You changed the rules of the game every time you played it. I can't please you. I can't. Nothing will ever be enough. So sad. Poor old Dad, deprived of his little pleasures. Well, you killed them, you killed them, you...

Dr Milton flinches at the look of venom that crosses his daughter's sulky face. He restrains himself with difficulty. He congratulates himself and the Mothers that Matti has been handed the challenge of a Blue Ribbon this year. Another year, tougher than all the rest, of discipline and responsibility and application, and she will be compliant. She must be. He will not give up until she is.

TWENTY-FIVE

Dr Milton himself delivers Matti back into the eternal February scene. Queen's Square is awash with returning girls.

'This is it, Matti. Give it your best shot. Mmm?' Dr Milton turns around in his seat and leans over to open the back door for his daughter. She leans towards him and kisses him briefly, takes her case and gets out of the car. She walks towards the crowd, the excited, noisy mass and it barely touches her. She reads the usual lists, registers her name and room number and moves slowly up the stairs. Another year, the room might have delighted her. Now all she feels is the most profound relief at the solitude granted her. Her room, under the bell tower, with the long windows and the huge old-fashioned bathroom that is hers and hers alone. Quietly she closes the door, putting the school behind her. She sits on the bed and stares out at the harbour. It spreads out before her eyes, shimmering, glacial. She narrows her eyes against the clarity and breathes deeply. Alone, alone, alone.

'Matti! How lovely to have you back with us once more!' The girl jerks back into the world. Mother Anton stands before her and before Matti can rise and curtsey, the nun bends and plants a dry kiss on her cheek. 'Well, my dear, this is a big and important year for you, isn't it?' Matti nods. 'You are all precious to us, you and your classmates. But you, Matti, are our oldest child. You've been with us the longest. How many years is it? Twelve! So you are extra special. I know this year is a very arduous one for you girls coming up to your final exams but you can rest assured that the

150

Community and I will do everything we can to help you all. Do you like your room?'

'Yes Mother. It's lovely. Thank you.'

'Good. Good. But not too much sitting staring out the window. We can't have you being distracted, can we?' The nun laughs, a dry, uncomfortable sound, as if she has had small practice in the art. 'Well, my dear, I must get downstairs and help supervise. There is so much to do when the newcomers arrive. I do like to get round to say hullo to my upper first, though, and have a few words with them. Perhaps, after dinner, when everyone is more settled, you might pop along to my room for a little word. Welcome back, Matti.' A beam of warmth has entered the silent girl. 'Matti' she had called her!

The nun turns and walks away. Matti sits quite still. The kind words have disarmed her. Horrid, snuffling tears run down her face. *Love me, please love me. Is there someone who will protect me?* The dinner bell rings. Matti washes her face and goes to join the rest of the school.

When Queen's Square is cleared and quiet and the rest of the school is upstairs unpacking and preparing, she is summoned to Mother Anton's room. It smells of floor polish and gleams austerely but the nun smiles widely so that the harshness of her features softens and she ushers Matti in.

'Sit down, Matti.' Matti perches uncomfortably on the oak stool. 'Well, my dear. I am sure we are going to work well together. Now, I know this is a difficult year. You girls have the pressure of exams, but also the pressure of knowing that soon you will leave the protection of the convent and have to start making your way in the world. I have no doubt that every Sacre Coeur girl can do this. We do not prepare you here for the life of a contemplative. We prepare each and every one of you to take her rightful place in society, contributing her own unique skills. Have you thought, Matti, where you wish to apply your skills?'

'Yes, Mother.'

'Really, my dear? And where is that?'

'I want to go to the National Institute of Dramatic Art, Mother. I want to act.'

'Oh. And have you talked this over with the family?'

'I've tried to, Mother.'

'And?'

'Well...'

'I see. I can understand, Matti. You are talented in that direction. We have all enjoyed your performances over the years. But, my dear, it is a life fraught with temptation. I can understand that your parents would be concerned. What's more, it is not a secure life, Matti. Like your parents, we are assuming that you will be going on to the university and getting a solid degree behind you. Perhaps then might be a better time to decide if you are still interested in acting. Anyway, my dear, we can talk about this later on.

'Before you go off to bed, there's one more thing. It is customary for our Blue Ribbons to join the Children of Mary Sodality and wear the medal.'

'Oh, Mother, I would be insincere if I did. I don't feel...'

'Feel? What has feel got to do with it?'

'I believe in God, Mother...'

'Thank goodness for that!' Mother Anton is not above irony.

'I don't know where He is in my life. I don't understand anything any more.'

'My dear, it is not for you to understand. Ask His help, Matti. Batter down the gates of heaven with your prayers. Join the Sodality and Our Blessed Mother will help you too.'

'Not yet, Mother. But I will think it over.'

'Matti, Matti. I fear you will be carried through the gates of heaven kicking and squealing every hard-fought inch of the way, but through you will go. Off to bed now, and remember, Our Blessed Lord grinds to dust those who He will make clay in His hands. Good night and God bless you, my dear.'

Matti curtseys. She longs to speak, to be enfolded, hidden. But there are no words for the things she wants to say, the creeping, sinister, terrible things that uncurl and flex in her brain. She leaves the room. The corridors are empty and dark and quiet. Only her footsteps echo in the space. She passes through the heavy baize doors and crosses in front of the chapel where the nuns are chanting Vespers. She pauses a moment, genuflects, *help me*, and moves on, up the stairs, up to her refuge.

The order of life in the convent reasserts itself. More withdrawn than she has ever been, Matti prepares for the final exams.

One Sunday morning she has a surprise meeting. There, waiting for her at the bus stop, is Flynn. Looking nothing like the Flynn she can ever remember, but definitely Flynn. The two girls hug and kiss.

'Oh, Flynn, I have missed you so much. I really have. It's wonderful to see you. How are you?'

'Okay. I've got a home weekend from the jail so I had to come and see me old mate.' They walk a little way from the bus stop to the tree-lined, more private street that branches off, and sit on an old stone wall.

'You look wonderful Flynn, all the make-up and everything. Do your parents let you?'

'Well they can't really stop me, can they?'

'My parents would.'

'Well, mine don't. I think they're just so relieved to find some nuns that would take me for the year that they're prepared to overlook anything. Poor old Mum. I'm a bit of a trial to her, I suppose.'

'I suppose so too,' Matti laughs. 'Oh, Flynn, it's really gorgeous to see you.'

'And how are you getting on, eh? Still topping all the tests, and a Blue Ribbon, I bet.'

'Well...'

'Come on, Matti, that's great. I admire you so much. I always have, you know. You're a real trier. You've got what they say I have none of. Discipline. Good on you.' Matti looks at her friend and loves her. No scorn, no judgement. Plain, unadulterated good nature.

'Oh, I wish you were still with us.' Flynn looks exotic, rich and wonderful, like some strange bird of paradise with multicoloured streaks in her hair. 'Are you allowed to have your hair like that?'

'Course not. But what can they do? It won't wash out for a few weeks so they'll have to put up with it.'

'But be careful, Flynn. What happens if they expel you?' Flynn shrugs. 'What's in your bag. Can I look?' It is a bulging carpet bag.

'Sure. Not much. Oh, there are some neenish tarts in that white paper bag. Thought you might like some.' Matti scrabbles about and draws them out and they munch together. Matti examines the bag's contents. 'Oh Flynn. Do you smoke?'

'Yeah. When I can.'

'Oh, and what's this? A lolly?'

'Oh, Matti. For heavens sake. Don't you know what that is? Haven't you ever seen one before? It's a tampon. You know, you shove it up yourself instead of wearing those terrible pads.' Matti examines it.

'Oh. I've never seen one before. But I thought, you know, well, virgins can't use them, can they?'

'Dunno. S'pose not. Dunno really.' Casual Flynn. 'I've got a tat, too.'

'A what?'

'A tattoo.'

'You haven't!'

'I have. Want to see?' Matti nods. Speechless. Flynn winds her sleeve right up to her shoulder and turns slightly. There is the tiny tattoo.

'Flynn! What's it meant to be?'

'It's a Manxman.' Flynn rolls her sleeve back down. They eat another neenish tart. And then the idea comes to Matti, an idea of startling boldness.

'Flynn, I've decided about next year. I'm going to NIDA. You know, the National Institute of Dramatic Art.'

'Good on you.'

'Will you help me with something?'

'Sure.'

'Look, I don't want anyone to know at this stage, because they'll try to stop me. I know they will. I have to present it as a fait accompli. Will you write for entry forms from your place in my name and ask them to send all the details to you and then in the holidays you can give them to me?'

'Course I will. No probs. No one ever opens anyone else's mail at our place. It'll be fine.'

'Flynn, you're wonderful. Promise you won't forget!'

'I won't.'

'Hey! Look at the time. I better go. They'll be waiting at home wondering where I've got to.' They hug again and Matti moves off up the hill. She looks back once to wave. Flynn is sitting on the wall, swinging her legs.

Flynn gets all the papers and turns up in the back of the church one Sunday during the holidays and smuggles them to Matti after Mass.

'I don't want you having anything to do with that girl,' says Mrs Milton. 'She's a disgrace.'

At night, in her room under the bell tower, Matti prepares her pieces for the audition. St Joan, Katharine from Henry V and a chorus piece from Oedipus. She has never felt more confident about anything. This is it!

In the September holidays, holidays marked by long tedious days of study, the exams being so close now, Matti tells her father the first lie she has ever told him in her life.

'I have to go to a Children of Mary meeting today. It's this afternoon.' And off she goes, the enormity of what she is doing filling her with adrenalin and determination and dread, for there will be a reckoning. No doubt about that.

She meets Flynn on the campus. Together they go to the theatre where Matti is to audition. She performs. She is confident. It will come out all right. It must. It must. It must.

Reality comes racing in one Sunday morning three weeks into the final term. She catches the tension in the air as she arrives home. It is palpable and alarming and she feels the familiar symptoms creeping upon her, the heat that threatens to explode her skull, the tightness of her aching neck, the churning belly.

'After lunch, Matti, I would like to see you in the formal room.' Matti looks at her father. He is furling and unfurling a long brown envelope. Barely contained agitation pulsates from his bulk. Better to have it out now.

'What for, Daddy?'

'You deceitful girl. You heard me. After lunch. In the formal room.' Such a meal. She goes through the motions, helping serve out, chewing on food that is dry and tasteless in her mouth. Meanwhile, Dr Milton questions her brothers on the minutiae of their lives and she knows that she does not exist, so potent is his exclusion. 'In his letter Desmond told us . . .' Matti tries to block out his words. St Desmond, the little priest-to-be. She misses him acutely; she hates him for being canonised in this house.

After the meal she approaches her father.

'Help your mother in the kitchen. I am taking the boys out for a run. I expect you to be waiting when I return.' Waiting! Why always the waiting? To make her more scared? To show how powerful he is? To call the shots? The bully! She goes to the kitchen in an agony of waiting. She is going to have to defy him and battle him and win, and it seems impossible that she can do so. She appeals to her mother. Perhaps . . .

'What is he going to say to me?'

'No, Matti. Your father can deal with you. You are underhand and deceitful and sly. I wash my hands of you. Your father can deal with you.' Hasn't Mrs Milton had to put up with his fulminating and his displeasure all week? Wouldn't she do anything for a quiet life? Yet Matti interferes, with her plans and her plots to escape and her rebellion against the status quo.

'Please . . .'

Her mother shakes off her daughter's arm. 'And go and comb your hair out of your eyes at once.'

The isolation hits the girl with renewed force. Tears of frustration and fear prickle her eyes.

'Stop that nonsense. Crocodile tears. Oh, you're a great little actress, Matti.' Her mother's voice is full of scorn and dislike. 'Go away. Go and wait for your father.'

And a horrible thing happens. Matti, who is so scared and lonely, laughs. From some perverse, disturbed, hysterical part of her a hooting laugh breaks out that she is unable to quench. Her mother hits her hard across the face and Matti flees the kitchen.

The formal room is stilted and cheerless, ridiculous Dresden shepherds and shepherdesses arranged along the mantelpieces and whatnots. She waits and the afternoon drags by. One hour. Two hours. Finally he comes. She hears the laughter and the banter and the rush of footsteps and she hears him peel off and come towards her. He enters and she sees the grim set his lips and the icy anger in his eyes spears into her.

'Stand up,' he commands. 'What is the meaning of this?'

He holds out the envelope. She goes to take it. He pulls it back.

'I asked you the meaning of this. I warn you, Matti. I am a tolerant man but my patience is running out.'

'What is it?' she whispers.

'You know as well as I do.'

'I don't.'

'You do. I'm warning you for the last time.'

'Is it from NIDA?' she implores. Terror of what he is going to do to her forces her to submission and uncontrollable floods of guilt.

'We could have saved time and unpleasantness if you had said that in the first place. And why, may I ask, was it necessary to go about this in an underhand way?'

'Because . . . because I didn't think you would let me do it otherwise.'

'Ah.' It is an exhalation of breath, a long, satisfied exhalation. 'You see, Matti. You knew and you went ahead nevertheless. You simply confirm my belief . . .'

'But Daddy, please. I want to. This is my life. What did they say? Please.'

'Suffice for me to say, Matti, that I have already declined your place and the offered scholarship. You know perfectly well that your mother and I, as responsible parents, could not permit this.' He tears the envelope and its contents into tiny pieces, throws them into the empty grate and, striking a match, sets them alight. *I did not even see it, and it's my life*, she thinks, watching the flame curl and the paper blacken. *My life.*

'Look here, my dear. It is for your own good that I have taken these steps. I have also asked the chaplain from the university to come over a little later and talk to you. You will hear for yourself how absolutely unacceptable this place is. Remember, my dear, what profiteth it a man if he gain the whole world and loses his soul? You will sit down and listen to Father Cosgrove.'

'I won't.'

'I beg your pardon.'

'I won't.'

'You will, my dear. While I am master of my own house, you will do as I say. You will return to the convent tonight and have no more Sunday outings until the exams are over. You will apply yourself to your study and if you do not achieve the marks we know you are capable of, you will return next year and repeat your final year. You will strive to conquer your underhand and wilful ways. You will root out and eliminate this sullen and moody behaviour. If you work hard, you can expect, eventually—for nothing is gained without hard yakker—to get great satisfaction out of your studies. And Matti, I expect you to continue with the dramatics. I expect you to use the talents God has given you so that we can be proud of you. But as a hobby, a healthy and pleasant hobby. Then, perhaps. I can begin to forget the unhappiness you have brought upon this house with your selfishness. I do not wish to go over this old ground but you persist . . .'

'Persist in what?' She hears herself shouting.

'There is no need for raised voices, my dear. You know well what I refer to.'

'I don't. I don't. I've never known and I never will.'

'Then I can only suggest you do some very hard thinking about it now. Remain here and think it over. Let me know when you have reached some conclusions.'

'I just want you to let me run my own life. That's all. What's so selfish about that? You're the selfish one. And you're a bully. You want my life as well as . . .'

'That's enough!'

'No. It's true. You want me to do whatever suits you and your needs. Why should I always do it your way? I'm me, not you.'

He stands shaking his head ruefully at her. The mildness on his face rouses her to a fury. She feels her right hand rise and she knows she is going to hit him, hit that smug, smiling, knowing face to kingdom come, and she feels her hand moving. In the slow motion of her mind she feels her other hand rise and forestall the blow so that she is there before him, hands upraised, clasped as in prayer.

'It is no use appealing to me like that, Matti. You can't

hoodwink me, my dear. I am only saving you from a lonely life. You are without friends, Matti, and will continue to be while you persist in these ways.'

'Don't say that. It's not true. I have lots of friends. I have Flynn.'

'Flynn!' He laughs sourly.

'Yes. Flynn. What's wrong with her? Go on. Tell me.'

'Don't use that tone of voice with me, my girl.'

'Go on. Tell me.' Dr Milton shakes his head. 'Go on. Tell me.'

'Very well, if you persist. Flynn is a bad influence. You are absolutely forbidden to have further contact with her. Her behaviour with the Mothers has been continuously bad and...'

'How do you know?'

'I have my ways. Let me assure you, there is very little I don't know.'

'You think you're God, knowing everything. Well, you're not. And Flynn is my friend and she always will be.'

'Be that as it may, it is now the end of the friendship. Birds of a feather... Matti. That is another reason you will remain at the convent until the term ends.' He pauses. 'Friends?' Matti's head shoots up in disbelief. 'Friends?' He asks again and holds out his hand.

She stares at him. Anger and hatred are galloping helter-skelter up her spine into her brain. She sees the prisoners on the rack kissing the instruments of torture. *Hate. Hate. Spittle and bile and stench. I will split apart if I cannot stop this expulsion of vomit. How can I ever come back if this evil is let loose to crawl upon the floor?* Burning, freezing, trapped in her cave, slowly, with averted eyes, she extends her hand.

'Now, now, Matti. With a good grace. Remember our little chat. Let's not have words again. Remember, dear, I'm on your side.'

He takes her hand, shakes it, cuffs her gently on the side of her head and hurries from the room. Matti stands very still, allowing the turbulence, the sour disgusting things, to subside. *Still. Still. Still. One false move and they will spew everywhere and the stench, the slime, will never be obliterated.* She stands motionless. She has no idea which way to move again.

TWENTY-SIX

Mother Anton watches her upper first closely in their final term. She knows they are wont to overdo things as the pressure of exam preparation mounts. She sees that they have boiled eggs for breakfast and a tonic before tea. They have hot milk before bed and she patrols the rooms and checks under their mattresses for torches and study notes. She watches them closely. But not closely enough.

Matti holds up the dormitory pass and the nun on surveillance in the study room nods. Matti walks quickly upstairs, her heart beating fast, her temples pounding. She is almost overwhelmed with anxiety. She knows how to dispel these feelings but she needs privacy and cannot always wait until night falls and she is alone with her soft cushion of pins in the dark and the peace. The pounding seems to fill her chest. Her entire body throbs with distress. Her neck stings with tension. Escape. Escape.

She walks into her room, closes the door firmly behind her and sits upon the bed. She stares out at the harbour and starts to rock. Sometimes this rocking is enough to calm her and she needs do nothing else. Hypnotically, rhythmically, she rocks back and forward, counting slowly, automatically, to herself. She holds her arms close to her body, wrapping herself in the protection of herself, unable to touch or feel beyond herself. All around her, pressing in upon her, drawing her out into its spaces, is the gleaming ice field, like plate glass, flawless and terrible. Matti rocks gently. She must not disturb the ice or the bottomless ravines will open about her. Gently, gently, rock and rock.

But before the calm comes, the tea bell clangs and she hears herself gasp with fright. How can she go down while this hotness, this fear, still grips her, the metal jaws of the trap snapped shut upon the nape of her neck? With intense weariness she reaches into her cupboard and draws out a small bottle of liniment that she keeps there. She dips her index finger into the greasy mass and, standing very still, carefully touches the finger to both eyeballs. The sting makes her gasp with pain. Her eyes water, trying to reject and wash out the liniment. Ruthlessly, calmer already, she inserts more, forcing herself to stare, wide-eyed, into the shimmering mirages of the distance. Now her eyes are bloodshot and streaming, the burning and searing almost overwhelming her. Her stomach heaves in waves of nausea. She rushes to the bathroom. The pain makes her vomit. As the retching and gagging subside, she stands straight, calm now and with head bowed she walks back to the study room, deposits the pass and joins the ranks for the dining room.

She sits without speaking throughout the meal and her table mates look at her swollen lids and weeping eyes and wonder. Casually. After all, she is upper first and there are a lot of tears from them these days with exams so close.

Friday afternoon. Mother Anton is taking a quiet stroll through the bush. She has urged a tennis round robin on her girls.

'Off you go now. Work up a sweat. Clear the cobwebs. No one may sit at her desk until after tea tonight. Off you go.' And Mother Anton has taken herself off too. She needs it as much as they. Her duties are onerous and she rarely gets the chance for a break. So, she strolls towards the promontory, the dangerous rocky outcrop with the placid harbour beaches at its base. She will find a boulder to sit on and say her rosary there, uninterrupted, for it is strictly out-of-bounds to the girls except for feast-day *cache-cache*. Who is this then, huddled in the lee of the rocks, staring out across the harbour? Mother Anton quickens her pace and claps her hands in a peremptory fashion.

'Who's that there? Who is it? Matti!' She has reached the girl's side. 'Whatever are you doing here? You're supposed to be out at the fields.' The girl does not move or acknowledge the nun in any way. 'Matti!' She shakes her by the shoulder and the girl turns slowly and stares at her. 'Matti, whatever are you doing? You should be with the others.' The girl continues to stare at her. Mother Anton stares back. 'Matti, get up at once.' She stretches out her hand to help the girl. Matti struggles dizzily to her feet, her face expressionless. She seems to be battling to focus her eyes.

'My dear . . .'

'I'm sorry, Mother, I don't know . . .'

'How long have you been here, Matti?' The girl shakes her head, unable to answer. A frisson of alarm runs through the nun. The girl's face. As if a cog were missing, a vital life spark in a unique machine. These exams! They put too much pressure on the girls. 'Never mind, dear, never mind. But you must not be going off by yourself. It's not a good example to the others. We'll walk back together, shall we, and perhaps we can get you a cup of tea in the scullery.' She tucks her arm into Matti's and pats her hand affectionately. Off they go, the nun and her weary child. Mother Anton sees the girl turn her head in a curious slow way and stare at her, her eyes lost and sad. *If I leaned all my weight on you, would you hold me up? If I leant on you would you help me walk along?*

'Here we are now, dear. Drink that up. You're over-tired. Exams start next week. You mustn't get run-down. No late study for you, my girl, and remain in bed for a Second Rise each morning. We can't have you getting sick before the exams, can we?'

The hall is set with rows of desks, the curtains have been adjusted to keep out the strong morning sun. Strangers sit around the walls on fold-down chairs, old women with knitting bags, shaky old men with nicotined fingers that itch to roll a fag. Now the girls start to arrive, the nuns giving them last minute advice at the door and pushing them through with a prayer and a word of encouragement. The Education Department representatives start to hand out papers. Day after day it has been going on and this is the last paper of all.

'You have ten minutes reading time. No student may start to write until the ten minutes are up. You may now turn over your papers.' There is a flurry of movement and the tension lessens. Silence. Concentration. Then the time bell rings. They start to write, the flowing Sacre Coeur hand degenerating as they scribble through book after book. All the facts and figures, theories and philosophies, diagrams and charts that they have memorised are regurgitated upon the paper, the cumulus of their learning.

Only Matti has not yet started to write. She stares in confusion at the questions before her. The paper shines blindingly up at her and she squints. 'You will apply yourself to your study and if you do not achieve the marks we know you are capable of, you will return to the convent next year and repeat... And Matti, I expect you to continue with the dramatics. It is a pleasant and healthy hobby.' Matti stares over the heads of the supervisors at the closed curtains of the stage. She grits her teeth and her body shakes in panic. Hopelessly, she picks up her pen.

Three hours pass. Time is almost up. Matti stares at the pages, trying to read over her work. There it is, page after page of filled space. Her mind refuses to obey her, her eyes barely focus. She is unable to read what she has written. She wonders if she has written anything at all. Perhaps it is an illusion. Surely not. Hasn't she put down there everything she has ever learnt about the subject? Yet she cannot decipher it. She stares at the scrawls. She narrows her eyes to bring the words into focus. Sweeps and swirls and curlicues and dots, enlarging and fading before her eyes. It is useless, she cannot read whether it is English or gibberish, whether it is sanity or nonsense. She closes the books and sits back in her chair, to wait.

Dr Milton waits. He has been waiting a long time now. He has watched the upper first come streaming out of their last exam into the promise of a sunny world, all talking at once, tossing books in the air, kissing the nuns, hugging each other, stumbling over their luggage, calling, promising, bursting to be gone. He waits. The crowd lessens, the noise subsides. Matti does not come. Dr Milton looks at his watch, frowns and strides towards the Queen's Square door. Where he meets Mother Anton.

'Good afternoon, Mother. I am waiting for Margaret-Anne. Have you seen her? The others have been and gone.'

'Oh, I'm so sorry, Doctor. Perhaps she has gone to say goodbye to some of the younger ones. We'll get her for you at once.' She signals to a young novice.

'Mother, could you go along and look for Margaret-Anne? Her father is waiting. I'll go along myself, Doctor. Just a moment.'

She moves off and climbs up to Matti's room. It is empty. The cases and the old mohair rug stand in readiness beside the bed. The mattress stands on its side and the bedclothes are folded neatly. Mother Anton checks the bathroom. Empty. Away she goes, down the Tower Stairs. She hears running footsteps.

'Mother?'

'Yes, Mother. I've found her...'

'Tell her to come at once. Her father is... The two nuns come face to face in the gloom at the turn of the stairs. The words die. Mother Anton follows the nun.

In a dark corner of the Tower Stairs she finds the girl.

'Matti! Matti!' The girl does not move. Her eyes stare dully out at the frozen wasteland. Blood and ice and distance have become one. 'Mother, ask Dr Milton to come at once. Quickly. I'll wait here.' She crouches over the still, cowering figure, crooning. Dear God, dear God. Her eyes follow the raking, terrible strokes. She holds the bloody hand. She cradles that insane lost face against her own black habit.

There is a clattering of running feet. The nun looks up at Matti's father, speechless, beseeching. He looks down at his daughter, bewilderment, pain, disbelief in his eyes. He bends as though to fold himself over her but pulls back rigidly and stands straight and unrelenting. His voice croaks in despair. He clears his throat.

'Sow the wind, Matti, and you reap the whirlwind,' he says, to anyone who is still listening.

TWENTY-SEVEN

So this was it. This was what Margaret had come for. To face her father and replay their life together once more and see what power he still had over her. To test once and for all if she could stand alone, adult and strong and healthy and not need him and the past to affirm her existence. She entered the bathroom, quickly stripped off her clothes and showered away the exhaustion of the night. A toothbrush stood in a mug. She hesitated momentarily then loaded it with paste and scrubbed her teeth. *He wouldn't mind. He's past minding now and I don't mind. We're part of each other, aren't we?*

When she emerged he was awake and the sister was giving him another of the injections that he had had throughout the night. Her father was watching her. He seemed alert and rested.

'Come here, dear. Come here.' She hurried over. He gestured feebly to the wall. 'It's an extraordinary thing. See that picture? Can't understand how they do it. See? The two Chinamen. Look at it from the side. See? Moving like that. Clever, eh? See, smoking away. See the smoke moving down?' She followed his eyes and looked back at him. He looked so pleased at his magic picture. 'D' you see?'

'Well, not really. It's a picture of camellias, Daddy. You know. Flowers.'

'Yes, well, maybe they are. But the Chinamen are there too.' She sat down beside the bed. Again his hand snaked out from under the bedclothes and sought hers. She took it and let it lie tiredly in hers.

'What am I doing here, dear?'

165

'You're sick, Daddy.'

'No, no, no, no, no. How did I get up here?'

'Where?'

'Here. To Brisbane. I haven't been able to drive for a long time. Who drove?'

'You're not in Brisbane.'

'Then, where am I?' There was anguish and confusion in the sunken eyes.

'It's all right, darling. You're in hospital. I'm here with you. The others will be here soon.'

'Terrible. Terrible mess. On the night path.'

She looked at him and felt the horror rising. *No, don't let him be like this. It's unbearable. Die. Please die.* But he didn't stop. He couldn't stop. His voice tumbled on and on in manic nonsense and he sought her explanation and verification. She nodded and assented and could make no pattern of the mumbo-jumbo. Let there be quiet, she prayed, clasping the hand tighter. And suddenly he seemed to rise up in the bed. He leaned over and patted her leg firmly.

'Good strong thighs,' he said, quite clearly. Then he lay back on the pillow and closed his eyes. Those were the last words he ever said.

She looked at his face. Something had changed. His head had fallen to the side, his mouth was open and from it came a deep gurgling sound. A rattle. The death rattle. She knew this at once. It had to be. It wouldn't be long now. Soon he would be dead. It would be finished. *Oh, Daddy.* She leaned over and, as to a sleeping baby, she started to pat his soft white hair. He couldn't stop her now. She could do whatever she wanted.

And even when her mother and brothers arrived, she stayed where she was, at the head of the bed, patting him. On and on through the day he laboured, battling for breath through the terrible rattle. Only once she spoke. To ask the sister if he was in pain. If this struggle was as terrible as it seemed. And no, she was told, he would not be aware any more. Just to be sure, though, they injected the drug, every ten minutes now.

The room was full. Family, nuns, old friends, all needing to be there somehow to offer safe passage. She was aware that Desmond stood with his arm around his mother's shoulder. In a remote, detached way she was glad of this and grateful to her brother. Every few minutes someone approached the dying man and pushed a tube down his throat and there was a choking sucking noise and dirty brown material, the mess of decay, flowed away. Leave him alone, she wanted to cry. Leave him alone. Let him die. Surely it can't matter. But it was done so gently, with small murmurings and tenderness, that she turned away her head.

It doesn't matter any more. We have lived. We have tried. We have done our best. I didn't die, Daddy. I wanted to tell you I forgave you. But I didn't because you didn't know you needed forgiveness. And, if that was so, could I hold you responsible? And now you're dying and I see you, struggling like me. One day I too will die, but not yet awhile. One day, perhaps, we'll meet merrily in heaven. Then you'll know everything. And so will I. But now, we understand so little. I can wait.

Some time the change came. To her imperceptible. But an old nun who was sitting in the corner began to pray aloud.

'Hail Mary, full of grace, the Lord is with thee. Blessed art thou amongst women and blessed is the fruit of thy womb, Jesus. Holy Mary, Mother of God, pray for us sinners, now and at the hour of our death. Amen.' Hail Mary... Holy Mary... Hail Mary... Holy Mary... On and on it went. The body on the bed no longer struggled against the rattle. It was quieter, the breaths spaced longer and longer. Margaret moved. She sat on the bed and took the poor, tired old head in her arms. It rested there. Quieter and quieter. Hail Mary... Holy Mary...

'Pray for us sinners, now and at the hour of our death. Amen.' On and on it went like a mantra. Margaret's lips moved. The sound flowed over them hypnotically. On and on. 'Pray for us sinners, now and at the hour of our death. Amen.' She cradled the head that she had hated and loved and feared almost unto death. Tears flowed down her cheeks and she did not care. She was overwhelmed with pity for this man who had tried so hard and got it wrong so often but who, by the very act of his dying, had given her this chance to face him once more and know that along with the hate she could let herself love him and not be annihilated.

He gave one last, long, sighing breath. He was dead.